SCORCHED SECRETS

A CHRISTIAN ROMANTIC SUSPENSE

FINNEGAN FIRST RESPONDERS

LAURA SCOTT

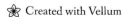 Created with Vellum

CHAPTER ONE

Emergency department physician Faye Kimble squinted against the bright sunlight piercing the horizon as she walked to the parking garage on aching feet. She hated working night shift. Sleeping during the day was unnatural. Her body clock thought that when the sun was up, she should be awake too. The good news was that after working five days straight, all of them twelve-hour night shifts, she had the upcoming weekend off. Three long, glorious days.

Was it pathetic that all she wanted to do was stay at home, sleep, eat, and binge-watch shows from her favorite streaming service? Yeah, she needed to get a life.

Stifling a yawn, she headed down the cement stairs to the lower level of the parking garage. This was the area with designated physician parking spots. An orange glow at the end of the aisle up ahead made her frown.

Was that a fire?

She rubbed her eyes, wondering if her sheer exhaustion was making her see things. The summer months were always the busiest for the Trinity Medical Center Emergency Department, and she'd lost track of the number of patients she'd seen over the past twelve hours. Over the past five days, each blending into the next.

When she opened her eyes, the orange ball was still there. Flames shooting up from the interior of a car. Taking a few steps forward to see better, she frowned.

Her car!

Her previous exhaustion faded as she called 911 to report the fire, then contacted the hospital security department. While she waited for both the security guards and the fire department to arrive, she searched frantically for a fire extinguisher. Shouldn't there be one on every level?

Then again, the parking garage was all concrete and steel. Nothing flammable.

Except the cars themselves.

Faye had no idea how long she stood dumbly staring at the fire burning inside her car. It took a moment for her to realize one of her car windows had been broken, providing oxygen to fuel the flames. Hospital security arrived first, with the sound of fire truck sirens a close second.

"What happened, Dr. Kimble?" Calvin asked. Many of the security staff knew her by name as they often were called to the emergency department to help with rambunctious and sometimes dangerous patients.

She waved her hand at the relatively contained fire. "I have no idea. I came out here to see that." A thought occurred to her. "We'll need to check the camera video feeds; there's no way this fire started inside my vehicle by accident."

Security officer Calvin Richter reached up to speak into his radio, sending the request to save the video to his dispatcher. Faye knew very well the medical center had literally hundreds of cameras set up in strategic locations around the campus. Not in patient rooms, but nearly everywhere else.

The fire had to be the work of a prankster, but the fact that her car was targeted nagged at her. Her car wasn't expensive like those driven by the senior medical staff, especially the surgeons. Glancing around, she saw a cherry-red Corvette convertible, a couple of BMWs, and a Lexus. Her vehicle was a ten-year-old Chevy sedan.

Was it possible the person who'd done this knew she was the eldest daughter of Fire Chief Dorian Kimble? Maybe someone had a grudge against her dad.

No, they would target his car, a much nicer one than hers. Wouldn't they?

The wailing sirens grew louder now, making it impossible to speak. Calvin drew her away from the fire as a set of firefighters came down the stairwell hauling a long hose. Seeing the flames, they didn't hesitate to run toward the fire.

Faye watched with admiration as the crew went to work. When she was younger, she'd thought of becoming a firefighter like her dad but discovered she not only hated the physical training required, but she couldn't have completed it even if she'd wanted to. Thankfully, her science scores were off the charts, enabling her to graduate from high school early and obtain a scholarship to college where she'd majored in premed. Her dad claimed he was still proud of her, but she thought he was a bit disappointed she hadn't followed in his footsteps.

But there were plenty of brave men and women who worked for him. Like those she watched now. Thankfully, it didn't take the crew long to get the fire under control, but from where she stood, it looked as if the entire interior of her car was nothing but a black, lumpy mess.

No question the fire had been set on purpose. But why?

"Faye?" One of the firefighters came over to stand beside her. She recognized him as Colin Finnegan. She'd grown up in Brookland near the Finnegan family; her father's house was only two blocks away. They were the same age and had gone to the same high school. They'd never dated, but she'd always admired him and the rest of the Finnegan family. He placed a hand on her arm. "Hey, are you okay?"

"As much as I can be." She blew out a breath, striving to sound calm. "Thanks for responding so quickly."

Colin's brown eyes searched hers. "Faye, this fire was set on purpose, so I need to ask who might be upset with you. A patient? A family member? An ex-husband or boyfriend? Who would do such a thing?"

She shook her head helplessly, her knees feeling weak. She crossed over to sit on the bottom step of the concrete stairwell. "Possibly my ex-husband, Rory Owen. Although he isn't the fire-setting type."

Colin nodded thoughtfully, crouching beside her. His concern was sweet, but her previous exhaustion was returning with a vengeance. "Okay, that's a place to start. I've called our arson investigator, Mitch Callahan, to examine the scene."

She was familiar with the Callahans, too, because Mitch's wife, Dana, was one of their emergency department nurses, as was Colin's younger sister, Alanna Finnegan. There were rumors flying around about the Finnegans and Callahans being second cousins, which she'd found comical since both families were large on their own. Together they were larger than some towns.

"How long will that take?" Despite her earlier concerns about being able to sleep during the day, she wanted nothing more than to head home and crawl into her bed.

Colin's expression filled with compassion. "You look beat, but if you can hang on for a few more minutes, that would help."

"Sure." She offered a wan smile. "What's a few more minutes tacked on to the end of a long shift?"

He frowned. "If you'd rather go home, I'm sure Mitch can meet you there."

"No." She waved a hand. "I'm hoping to get some sleep when this is over." Although the more she thought about someone, maybe even Rory, setting a fire in her car on purpose, the less likely it seemed she'd be able to sleep.

Her divorce from Rory had been finalized well over a year ago. Despite Rory's cheating on her, he'd tried to convince the court that he should get ongoing financial support to the tune of half her salary. Since their marriage had only lasted two years, the judge did not grant him a dime of alimony. Especially with Rory's infidelity. They did split the equity in the house, which considering she'd made all the payments while Rory struggled to hold down a job, was enough of a gift.

While she had no doubt Rory still harbored a grudge against her, she had trouble imaging him sneaking into the parking garage to break her car window and start a fire. He'd be more of the type to take a baseball bat to the Chevy, smashing it to pieces. If he bothered to do anything at all.

"Oh, I almost forgot, there are cameras down here." She touched Colin's knee. "Calvin the security guard asked the hospital to save the video. That should help with Mitch Callahan's investigation."

"That's great news." He smiled. "We'll get you out of here ASAP."

She nodded, still ruminating over the fire. Maybe this wasn't anything personal. It was possible a couple of teenagers with too much time on their hands had come down here and picked a car at random.

But setting it on fire? That wasn't a typical prank. Stealing the car or simply vandalizing it was something that had happened before. This level of the parking garage was clearly labeled physician parking, which may have contributed to a teenager's rationale. Most people thought doctors were made of money, and while it was true that she was paid a nice salary, she also had student loans to pay off. Not to mention a mortgage on her small house. Her undergraduate degree had been mostly covered by her scholarship, but medical school was expensive.

Hearing footsteps coming down behind her, she pushed herself to her feet to move aside. A tall, blond-haired man nodded at Colin, then glanced at her. "I'm Arson Investigator Mitch Callahan."

"Faye Kimble." She shook his hand. "It's my car that was targeted."

"I heard." Mitch and Colin exchanged a long look. "Give me a minute to look at your vehicle, then I'll ask you a few questions."

She tried not to sigh. Colin followed Mitch to the vehicle. They spoke for a moment, then Colin joined his fire crew as they began winding up the hose and carrying it back up to the main level.

Since there were more people going up and down the stairs, she abandoned the steps to lean against the concrete wall to alleviate the pressure in her aching feet.

The firefighters disappeared, leaving Mitch Callahan to inspect the fire damage. Calvin came over to hold out his phone. "Dr. Kimble? We have the video feed here."

She took the device and pushed the play button. The parking garage was fairly well lit, but it still took her a minute to see the figure dressed in black from head to toe, a hoodie pulled up to hide his or her features. The figure darted toward her car, lifted a brick with a black-gloved hand, and smashed the window. Then the person set something in the car before turning and leaving.

She glanced up at Calvin. "Did you follow this person across the campus?"

"Yes, but he was on foot and disappeared out of range." The security guard grimaced. "I was hoping we'd get the guy's vehicle or his license plate number, but no luck."

"Thanks, Calvin." Other than the fact that the person who'd done this had gone straight to her car, the video wasn't helpful. The guy had his face covered, his head covered, and his hands covered. All they knew was that he was slender and roughly five feet, nine inches tall. "Will you send me a copy of the video? And you'll need to show this to Investigator Callahan."

"Will do." Calvin took his phone back and went over to join Mitch. Faye shifted her weight from one foot to the other, irrationally missing Colin's reassuring presence.

It was nice to have a familiar face nearby during a crisis. But of course, Colin was already heading out, returning to the firehouse with the rest of his crew. Besides, a damaged car was hardly life-changing.

After going through the video with Calvin, Mitch came over to ask her the same questions Colin had. "The only person who has been upset with me is my ex-husband, Rory Owen. But as I told Colin, he's not the fire-setting type of guy." She thought about the video, then added, "I guess the guy in the video could be him, but only if Rory had lost about thirty pounds."

"When did you last see Rory?" Mitch asked.

"At our final divorce hearing, just over a year ago." She

shook her head. "It seems odd he'd come after me now, a year after our divorce."

"Weren't you recently featured on the local TV news?" Mitch asked. "Dana mentioned you were working the night of the gas leak when five patients were brought in after suffering carbon monoxide poisoning. We saw a clip where you were interviewed on Monday."

"Yes, that's true." She frowned. "You really think Rory saw my brief moment of fame and thought, 'Hmm, I think I'll burn her car'?" She scoffed. "I doubt he even saw it."

"I'm open to other possibilities," Mitch said.

Her shoulders slumped. "I don't have any other ideas. Or enemies that I'm aware of. Maybe my dad has made someone upset?"

"It's possible. But then again, this arsonist has targeted you, not your dad." Mitch's expression gentled. "Go home to get some rest. If I have more questions, I'll call you."

"Okay." She gave him her personal cell number, then trudged back up the concrete stairs to ground level. Heading over toward the main emergency department doorway, she used her phone to access a rideshare. She was tired, hungry, and now she didn't even have a car to use on her three-day weekend off.

A spurt of anger hit hard. She didn't need the hassle of calling her insurance to report the fire and shopping for a new car.

If Rory was the mastermind behind this fire, she hoped Mitch found and arrested him very soon.

COLIN HUSTLED BACK to the hospital, glad to see Faye was standing near the front entrance to the emergency department. He pulled up alongside her and rolled down the passenger-side window of his Jeep. "Faye? Can I drive you home?"

She looked up in surprise. "Aren't you still working?"

"Nope. Our tour ended at eight. I knew you'd need a ride." He smiled reassuringly. "Come on, let me give you a lift home."

"Okay." She hit a button on her phone, likely canceling the rideshare she'd called, then opened the passenger door. When he pulled away from the curb, she sighed and rested against the seat. "Thanks, Colin."

"Anytime." He'd known Faye for years, but their paths had taken them in different directions. She'd graduated early from high school to attend college. He'd always known she'd end up doing great things. "Rough shift?"

"No worse than usual." She yawned widely. "I just finished five twelves in a row."

He whistled. "Sounds rough. Especially since I know you don't get much downtime."

"Not like you firefighters do, right?" She flashed a teasing smile. Her dark hair was pulled back in a ponytail, but strands had escaped and framed her face. "I hear you're all about the cooking."

"Hey, a man has to eat." He was used to the jokes about firefighters spending their time cooking and eating. He came from a family of nine kids. Two of his older brothers were cops, as was his older sister. He also had a brother in the FBI, a brother with the Coast Guard, and a brother with the National Guard. His sister Alanna was a nurse, and the youngest sibling, Elly, was an EMT.

Most of the time, he liked being the only firefighter in the family.

"I live along the Sunny Creek Parkway," she said. "I have a small house there."

"Okay." He glanced at her. "I didn't realize you had been married."

She wrinkled her nose. "As I said, I'm not anymore. And it was a mistake."

"Hey, we all make mistakes, Faye." He smiled reassuringly. "His loss."

"Yeah." She stared down at her lap for a moment. "I should have listened to my dad. He never liked Rory."

Colin nodded thoughtfully. He admired Fire Chief Dorian Kimble very much. The guy had been one of the reasons Colin had decided to study firefighting. Becoming a paramedic was part of the deal, and he'd found that aspect of the job interesting too. Truth be told, he preferred firefighting to taking care of sick people. "Your dad is a pretty good judge of character."

"Yeah, well, not when a girl thinks she's in love." She tucked a wayward strand of hair behind her ear. "That reminds me, I should call him. He'll hear about the car fire soon enough."

"I, uh, already let him know." Colin winced when she shot him a narrow look. "Come on, Faye, he's ultimately my boss. It's not like I could ignore the fact that the chief's daughter was targeted by an arsonist."

She groaned and closed her eyes. "Great. He's probably waiting at my place now."

"No, he's not. He mentioned heading into a meeting with the mayor, so that will keep him tied up for a while. He asked me to let you know that he'll swing by later."

"Of course, he will," she groused. "I'm fine, nothing that a solid eight hours of sleep won't cure. His time would be better spent with his family."

"His family?" Colin frowned at the term. "You don't get along with your stepmother?"

"Yes, Claire has always been wonderful. Their daughter, Annie, is great too. She's had a few boyfriend issues that has caused our dad's blood pressure to spike, but that's part of being a teenager." Faye waved a hand. "I was twelve by the time he and Claire were married, and Annie was born two years later. She's sixteen now and giving my dad more than a few gray hairs by rebelling against his house rules. She's driving now, too, which is giving my dad fits as well. Better that he's home with them than worrying about me."

"Checking on you is what any father would do." He thought about how his own family had grown closer over the more than ten years since their parents were killed in a terrible car crash. The oldest brothers, Rhy and Tarin, had moved home to help raise their younger siblings. The twins, Alanna and Aiden, had been seventeen at the time, and Elly had only been fourteen. Even now, all these years later, Rhy still checked in on them, especially if one of them tried to duck out of family dinner.

"Checking on me via phone is one thing, but there's no reason to stop by." She shot him a glance. "You did tell him I was fine, right?"

"Yep." Hearing fire truck sirens, he glanced around for the source of the blaze. "Wow, strange that they've gotten another call out so soon. Two fires in the span of a few hours is unusual."

"Colin?" Faye reached over to grasp his arm, the other hand pointing toward her passenger-side window. "Is that smoke?"

A curl of dark smoke lifted toward the sky. "Yes." They were too far away to pinpoint exactly where the smoke was coming from, but the general area was residential.

"A house fire?" She continued holding on to his arm as if needing the support.

"No way to say for sure." Car fires were more common in the summer, especially those cars that weren't well maintained. Lack of coolant often caused engines to overheat.

Different from the car fire that had damaged Faye's car. That fire had been started in the back seat, not the engine. The entire interior had been toast, and based on the year, make, and model, he felt certain her insurance company would consider it totaled.

They were heading in the same direction as the smoke, which gave him a bad feeling. He shot a glance at Faye, her gaze still lingering on the smoke.

"What if that's a house fire in my neighborhood?" Her voice was low and husky.

"We'll find out soon enough." The words had barely cleared his lips when the sirens grew impossibly loud. In his rearview mirror, he saw the fire rig he'd been on just a few hours ago coming up behind him.

Wrenching the wheel, he moved his Jeep over to the side of the road to give the fire truck room to pass by. A second rig came up next, along with an ambulance. All three vehicles sped past, intent on responding to the scene. The keen sense of dread grew worse as he pulled out to follow behind them.

Faye gripped his arm tightly. "Colin? Could it be my house?"

"Let's not jump to conclusions." He did his best to sound calm, but deep down, he feared she might be right. It would be a huge coincidence if one of her neighbors' houses started on fire less than an hour after her car had been targeted by arson.

He turned to head down Sunny Creek Parkway, then had to stop when the road was completely blocked off by the fire trucks. Shifting the Jeep into reverse, he backed up and then parked along the side of the road.

"It is my house!" Faye abruptly released him to push open her car door. The locks were still engaged, so she fumbled to hit the unlock button to get out.

"Faye, wait! We don't know that." He caught her hand. "Hold on, they're not going to let you get close to the scene. Wait here, I'll go and check things out."

"It's my house, see? I live in the white Cape Cod."

Feeling grim, he watched as firefighters surrounded the house, aiming their fire hoses at the blaze. There were several areas along the house where the fire had progressed, making him realize this was also the work of arson.

Sure, there could be an electrical fire, but he didn't think that was the case. No, just like the fire in Faye's car, this one had been deliberately set.

As if reading his mind, Faye whispered, "Why is this happening?" Her blue eyes were wide and tortured. "My car and my house? Why?"

"I don't know, but I'll find out." He squeezed her hand and jumped out of the car. He'd barely made it a few feet before an explosion rocked the earth.

He fell onto his hands and knees but quickly pushed up and kept going. His firefighter brothers and sisters were over there! The smoke was thicker now, making it impossible to see.

Coughing, he pulled the collar of his T-shirt up and over his nose and mouth to keep from inhaling so much of the thick smoke and soot. He didn't have any protective gear, and the blaze from the fire was hot on his skin. Raking his gaze over the area, he searched for his firefighter family.

Two guys emerged from the smoke, each carrying one of their fellow firefighters over their shoulders in the typical fireman carry. "This way," Colin shouted, gesturing for them to follow to the clearing in the road.

The firefighters gently placed their fellow firefighters on the ground to be examined. Colin took the one closest to him. Out of nowhere, Faye was there, too, examining the other firefighter.

Together they worked on his teammates, using rescue supplies from the ambulance. Even as Colin started an IV, then placed a breathing tube down Larry's throat, he silently prayed for God to save these two injured men.

CHAPTER TWO

Focusing on caring for the injured firefighters helped keep the shock and fear at bay. Faye diagnosed the firefighter she was working on with a concussion and what appeared to be a broken wrist. No other obvious signs of injury, but he'd need an abdominal and pelvic CT scan to be sure.

When the firefighter woke up and groaned, she couldn't hide her relief. The firefighter who'd carried him over had called him by name, so she used it now. "Mike? I'm Dr. Faye. You have a concussion and a fractured wrist, but you're going to be okay. Just rest here for a few minutes."

"What about Larry?" Mike peered up at her in confusion. "He was right beside me."

"I'm going to check on him now, but I need you to stay here." She patted his arm, then rose to her feet, stumbling over to check on the second firefighter. Colin looked up at her, his expression grim. "Larry hasn't woken up yet, and his pupils are unequal. I inserted an airway, but I'm concerned about him."

"Let me take a look." She used her phone flashlight to check Larry's pupils. Her stomach knotted with concern when she noted his left pupil was completely blown. She glanced over at the ambulance crew. "Get him transported to Trinity ASAP! I'll call to let them know he's on the way."

The crew jumped to do her bidding, lifting Larry up onto the stretcher, then wheeling him to the waiting rig. Moments later, he was tucked inside and on his way to the medical center.

True to her word, she called her colleagues to clue them in. "Injured firefighter on his way, severe head injury, left pupil blown. Make sure the neurosurgeon is available to take him to the OR."

"Understood," Dr. Murry said. "Thanks for the heads-up."

Faye lowered the phone, overwhelmed with guilt. Larry couldn't have been much more than twenty-five years old. And he could die because some heartless arsonist had targeted her house.

Why? That was the confounding question.

"Faye?" Colin's voice drew her from her thoughts. She stared at him, expecting to see anger in his brown eyes. She wouldn't be surprised if he blamed her for his colleague's injury. He looked grim but not angry. "Come with me."

"Where?" She turned to stare at the house. Or rather what remained of her house. There was damage to the properties alongside hers too. Would her insurance cover all of this? What if others had been injured, or worse?

"Come with me to the Finnegan homestead. You need to get some sleep."

Sleep? That was a laugh. "I won't be able to sleep. And why do you call your childhood home the homestead? I've always wondered about that."

"My parents started it, and we carried on the tradition."

He followed her gaze to the chaotic scene. "There's nothing more we can do here. The team has it under control."

He was right, but she didn't have to like it. Tearing her gaze away, she tried not to appear as dejected as she felt. "You may as well take me to a hotel."

"You won't get a room this early." He took her hand in his. "Is there a reason you won't go with me to the homestead? I promise my family will make you feel welcome."

Her exhausted brain couldn't come up with a good reason. Colin was being neighborly, and really, if anyone else in the Finnegan family, say Alanna, had made the offer, she wouldn't have hesitated. "Okay, I'll come with you for now. But I can't stay indefinitely." It would likely take months for her house to be repaired, if that was even an option.

Did insurance companies total houses the same way they did cars? She figured she'd find out very soon.

It was difficult not to think about how hard she'd worked to rebuild her life after her divorce. Taking her small bit of equity out of the sale of their joint home, she'd added a small nest egg from her savings to purchase the Cape Cod. She'd liked that house; it was small and cozy but all hers.

Now it was gone, just like her car.

Gone. Her knees threatened to buckle, but she forced herself to walk back to Colin's Jeep under her own power. Reminding herself they were material things helped keep things in perspective.

Yet it was impossible to ignore the sense of being violated. Her things weren't anything fancy or expensive, but they were hers.

Now they were a pile of ash.

"Hey, you're going to be okay." Colin slipped his hand

beneath her elbow as he guided her to the passenger-side door. "We're here for you."

"I know." It was nice to have friends like the Finnegans. She straightened her spine and slid into the Jeep. She wasn't sure sleep would come easily, but she hoped a few hours of rest would help her make sense of this.

When Colin jumped in behind the wheel, she glanced at him. "We'll need to call my dad and Mitch Callahan."

He nodded. "We will. Mitch can't do much at your place yet; the scene is too hot. But he'll be there tomorrow for sure." He grimaced. "Maybe this time you should call your dad."

She pulled out her phone and made the call. She ended up leaving a message, no doubt he was still in his meeting with the mayor. There were always budget issues when it came to police and fire services. Both were necessary, yet no one liked to pay more taxes to fund their civil servants.

"I keep coming back to the possibility this is related in some way to my dad, that someone is trying to get to me to hurt him." She abruptly straightened and picked up her phone again. "I should have thought of this before! I need to warn Claire and Annie."

"Good idea," Colin agreed.

Unfortunately, her stepmother didn't answer either. Not surprising. Faye liked Claire, but her stepmother made a career of going to the gym, shopping, having breakfast and lunch engagements, and generally doing nothing all day while staying away from home. Maybe Faye didn't understand it, but since Claire made her father happy, she kept her thoughts to herself.

After working five twelve-hour shifts straight, doing nothing all day sounded nice.

"Your dad will keep Claire and Annie safe," Colin

assured her. "I still think there is a personal vendetta behind these attacks. Are you sure there haven't been any contentious patient or family situations that we should be aware of?"

"Even if there were, I can't really discuss my patients with you or Mitch Callahan or anyone else." Patient privacy was a big deal in healthcare. "Besides, it's a rare day I don't have an irate patient or family member. But angry enough to do something like this? Setting fires to my car and my house?" She shook her head, fighting a wave of helplessness. "I can't even imagine anyone who would take such a drastic measure."

"I understand patient privacy, but this is serious." He scowled as he threaded through traffic toward Brookland. It felt odd to be heading to the neighborhood where she'd grown up. Especially since she hadn't lived there since heading off to college.

"You think I don't know that?" The image of Larry's blown pupil flashed in her mind. "I hate knowing Larry is suffering because of me."

"Not you, Faye. The arsonist."

"An arsonist carrying out a sick grudge against me." She couldn't hide the bitterness in her tone. "Same difference."

"Every firefighter goes in knowing the danger. This isn't your fault." He reached over to gently squeeze her hand. "Your dad would tell you the same thing."

She didn't agree, but arguing took too much energy. The brief adrenaline surge that had rejuvenated her when responding to the injured firefighters was fading fast.

When Colin pulled into the driveway of his childhood home, she was assailed by doubts. Why was she here? A hotel would be easier, no need for idle chitchat. With reluctance, she pushed her door open and stepped out of the vehicle. She must have been moving slow because Colin was already there, providing a helping hand.

"Are you hungry? Rhy's wife, Devon, likes to make breakfast."

"Not necessary. I'm more interested in sleep."

Colin stopped at the front porch to key in a code in the alarm. As he opened the door, he called, "It's me, Colin. I brought a guest, Faye Kimble."

"Come in," a female voice called. As Faye crossed the threshold, the scent of bacon, eggs, and coffee made her mouth water. Maybe she was hungry. "It's great to see you, Colin." A pretty, petite dark-haired woman smiled warmly. "We're always thrilled to have guests. And you're just in time for breakfast. Rhy is off today; he'll be down shortly."

"Thank you." She nudged Colin with her elbow, hinting he shouldn't mention her earlier statement. "Breakfast sounds lovely."

He flashed a smile, then keyed in the alarm code again. "Faye, this is Devon Finnegan, Rhy's wife. Devon, this is Dr. Faye Kimble, she works at Trinity as an ER physician."

"ED physician. Emergency department," Faye corrected. "ER is old language from when it was a single room with cubicles. We've come a long way from that."

"It's nice to meet you, Faye." Devon gestured toward the coffeepot. "Help yourself. I made it for Rhy and Elly since I'm only drinking decaf these days."

Faye wasn't sure why Devon mentioned the decaf until Colin asked, "And how is our future niece or nephew?"

"He's fine, thanks." Devon grinned. "The morning sickness is easing a bit, which is nice."

"He? I thought Rhy calls the baby she?" Colin teased.

"I'm right, he's wrong." Devon shrugged. "Either way, we're keeping the baby's gender a surprise until he's born."

Realizing Devon was pregnant only made Faye feel worse about imposing on them. Then again, breakfast had already been in the works when they'd arrived.

"No coffee for me either." Faye took another step into the room as Colin walked over to pour a cup. "I've had more than my fair share while working last night."

"Night shift is rough," Devon agreed. "Please sit, Faye. I'm sure you're exhausted."

"Thanks." She dropped into the closest chair as Rhy entered the room. He smiled at her, glanced curiously at Colin, then kissed Devon.

"Rhy, this is Dr. Faye Kimble. Faye, our oldest brother, Rhy."

"Nice to meet you." She smiled, trying not to wish they'd tried a hotel instead. "I appreciate your hospitality."

"Oh yes, Faye. You're Chief Kimble's daughter," Rhy said with a nod. "Always happy to help a neighbor."

"Sit down, Rhy, I have enough food for the four of us." Devon slid food onto four plates with the grace of someone who had made a living serving others.

The men sat, Colin choosing the seat next to hers. Rhy took Devon's hand, then bowed his head. "Dear Lord Jesus, we thank You for this food we are about to eat. We also ask that You keep our family and the Kimble family safe in Your care. Amen."

"Amen," Colin and Devon echoed.

Faye had been caught off guard by the prayer. Her family had attended church, mostly on special occasions, but it was clear the Finnegans lived their faith daily. Oddly, she was comforted by that thought.

She expected Rhy to ask Colin why she was there, but the conversation was centered around family stuff, like Quinn and Sami's upcoming wedding.

"You need to make sure you're off work, Colin," Rhy said. "I know it's not easy to coordinate our schedules, but Quinn really wants the family to be there. Especially since Sami doesn't have anyone to support her."

"I requested off, Rhy, that's all I can do." Colin sent her a sly wink. "Although maybe Faye can put in a good word with her dad. My boss won't deny my request for a weekend off if there's a directive from the top."

She chuckled. "Yeah, I can try, but don't pin your hopes on that. My dad leaves the managing of day-to-day operations to his captains."

"Hey, it's worth a shot," Colin joked.

She finished her meal before anyone else but was too tired to be embarrassed. Colin noticed, though, and rose to his feet. "Come on, I'll show you the guest room."

"Okay, thank you." She carried her dirty dishes to the sink, then turned back to face Rhy and Devon. "Thanks again. I appreciate your hospitality."

"Anytime," Devon assured her.

She followed Colin up the gracefully curved staircase to the second floor. He opened the second door on the right and gestured for her to step inside. "Get some sleep. We'll talk more about our next steps later."

"Okay, sounds good." It was only when she'd crawled into bed did she register his comment.

We'll talk about *our* next steps? She appreciated his kindness, but this wasn't his problem, it was hers.

Although honestly, she had no idea what to do about it.

———

"OKAY, COLIN, WHAT'S GOING ON?" Rhy pounced the minute he returned to the kitchen to finish his meal.

Swallowing a sigh, he met his brother's gaze. "Faye has been targeted by an arsonist."

The shock in Rhy's gaze, especially when he glanced at his pregnant wife, made Colin wince. "Okay, first of all, no one knows she's here. Secondly, both attempts took out her personal property, her car and her house. Faye hasn't been physically harmed by either fire."

"Her car and her house?" Devon echoed, her hand resting on her slightly rounded abdomen. "That's awful. I'm glad you brought her here, Colin."

"Does Chief Kimble know?" Rhy asked.

"He knows about the car, she had to leave a message about her house. He was meeting with the mayor." Colin took a bite of bacon and met Rhy's gaze. "I wouldn't have brought her here if someone had tried to kill her. I wouldn't put Devon in harm's way like that. But Faye worked five twelve-hour shifts in a row and was dead on her feet. I figured she'd be fine here for a few hours."

Rhy nodded, although there was still a shadow of concern in his gaze when he glanced at his wife. "I guess it's a good thing we have the security system and that I have the day off."

Colin finished his meal and pushed his plate aside. "Faye has an ex-husband, a guy by the name of Rory Owen. Mitch Callahan will likely be investigating both fires, but I figure it can't hurt for you to check this Owen guy out too. Apparently, their divorce was final over a year ago, but you might remember the major gas leak that brought several victims to Trinity. Faye was working that night and was interviewed by the local news about it."

Rhy frowned. "Your theory is that Owen resents her fame and fortune?"

Colin leaned back in his chair, spreading his hands

wide. "I don't know. If not her ex-husband, then who? I've already asked about angry patients or families. She doesn't think that's likely and won't breach patient privacy."

"Mitch will get a subpoena for any formal patient complaints against Faye. No lawsuits, huh?"

"Not that she's mentioned." He frowned. "I'm sure she'd know if there were any, right?"

"I assume so." Rhy sipped his coffee. "But we can find out for sure."

"Sounds like you're going to work on your day off." There was no anger or resentment in Devon's voice, but Colin still felt bad.

"No need, I can do the grunt work," he said quickly. "You two should enjoy your day."

"It's fine, we can shop for baby furniture another time." Devon waved a hand. "Family comes first."

Technically, Faye wasn't family, but he couldn't ignore her situation either. He met Rhy's gaze. "Why don't we do a little research before you go shopping? That shouldn't take too long."

"After you and I do the dishes," Rhy agreed.

"I can do it," Devon protested.

"Nope." Colin jumped to his feet. "We've got this."

"It's not like I can even enjoy another cup of coffee," Devon muttered glumly. "It's pathetic how much I miss it."

"Only sixteen weeks to go," Rhy teased.

Colin grinned as Devon groaned. It didn't take them long to wash and dry the dishes. When that chore was finished, Rhy led the way through the living room to the small alcove where he had a desk and computer set up.

"You should really use one of the bedrooms as an office," Colin said as Rhy sat.

"I would, but it seems like every time I turn around, one

of you is bringing someone here to stay for a while. Anywhere from a few days to several weeks." Rhy turned the computer on.

"I thought Sami and Quinn bought a house?"

"They did, but they don't close until the end of this month. They'll move in on September first." Rhy worked the keyboard for a few minutes. "No pending lawsuits against Faye." He typed again, then added, "No outstanding warrants against Rory Owen either."

"That doesn't mean he's in the clear." Colin didn't normally despise someone he'd never met, but from what little Faye had confided about her ex-husband, Rory deserved his ire. "This may be his first criminal venture."

"Maybe." Rhy glanced up at him. "Other than some bad debt, he's clean. I'm sure Mitch will question him, but you have to admit revenge is not typically a motive for arson."

"I get that." He frowned. "Ninety percent of arsonists are white males from twenty to thirty years of age. Owen fits right in there. Maybe he's been smart enough not to get caught before now?"

"Anything is possible, but you need more than his being an ex-husband to accuse him of a felony like arson."

"Yeah, yeah." Considering he was surrounded by cops, Colin understood well enough how the legal system worked. "I still think he's the prime suspect."

Rhy checked a few more things, then shrugged. "Nothing else is popping up here as interesting." He turned in the chair to face Colin. "You know, maybe Faye needs to think back to any patients she may have cared for who suffered minor burns. Could be the arsonist got too close to the flames, then became fixated on her when she cared for him."

"You're brilliant, Rhy. That's a good possibility." Colin

glanced toward the staircase leading to the second-story bedrooms. "I wish I'd have thought of that earlier. Not sure how long she'll sleep after working five night shifts in a row."

"Five night shifts? Brutal."

"Tell me about it." Colin shook his head, then grinned. "Faye puts me to shame. Makes my schedule look like a cake walk."

"Your schedule is a cake walk," Rhy shot back. "You don't work nearly as hard as the rest of us."

"Says who?" Colin lightly punched Rhy in the arm.

"All of us, Colin." Rhy laughed and stood, giving him a playful shove. "We all say that."

"You're just jealous because the general public likes firefighters better than cops." Colin glanced over when the front doorbell rang. He hoped it wasn't loud enough to wake Faye. "I'll get that. I'm sure it's Chief Kimble."

"How did he know Faye was here?" Rhy asked.

Colin noticed Chief Kimble standing on the porch through the window. "He doesn't, but he's here to talk to me anyway." After punching in the code, he opened the door. "Hi, Chief. Come in."

"Finnegan." Chief Dorian Kimble was a tall, imposing man, still physically fit despite his age being somewhere in the midsixties. Threads of gray running through his dark hair gave him a distinguished look. There had been some talk in the neighborhood when Chief Kimble had married Claire, who was fifteen years younger than him, but they seemed happy together. Colin figured it was no one else's business what their age difference was. "I got your message. What in the world is going on?"

"Please have a seat." Colin gestured to the kitchen table, realizing Devon had made her escape earlier. Rhy followed him in, so he made a quick introduction. "You remember my oldest brother, Rhyland."

"Of course." Dorian Kimble held out his hand to shake Rhy's. "I've always admired how you kids pulled together after your parents died."

"Thanks." Rhy always looked uncomfortable when given accolades about how he'd stepped in to keep the family together. To Rhy, it was just something that had to be done, there was no other option.

"If you and Devon want to head out to shop, that's fine." Colin wanted to give his brother the opportunity to leave. "I'll stick around."

"Okay, sounds good." Rhy nodded again at Chief Kimble. "Let me know if there's anything else either of you need."

"Will do." Colin crossed over to pour more coffee for himself and Faye's father. "How do you take your coffee?"

"Black is fine." Dorian shifted in his chair. "I don't like hearing my daughter's car and house were both started on fire. I have a call in to Mitch Callahan, too, but I know you were one of the first responders on scene."

"Just at the parking garage," Colin said. He sat across from Dorian. "You should know Faye is resting in one of the guest rooms upstairs after working several night shifts in a row."

"She is?" The chief's eyebrows levered up. "I assumed she went to our home."

Colin shrugged. "Devon had breakfast ready for us, so it worked out. Besides, I don't think she was able to reach Claire."

"Okay, that's fine." He didn't look surprised that Claire was out and about. "Tell me what happened."

Colin described the morning events in detail, starting

with the car fire and then discovering the second fire at her home. To his credit, Dorian didn't interrupt but waited until he'd explained everything, even the injury to the two firefighters and how Faye herself had jumped in to provide medical care to them.

"She's an amazing physician," Dorian said in a low voice. "I'm so proud of everything she's accomplished." Then he scowled. "Has anyone found her useless ex-husband yet?"

"No, but you should know Faye doesn't think setting fires is something Rory Owen would do." He shrugged. "I'm not saying that clears him, but she has a point. You and I both know that arsonists are a different breed of criminal."

"They are." The chief stared down at his coffee for a long moment, before lifting his gaze to his. "I think this is my fault."

Colin's gut clenched. "What do you mean?"

Dorian sighed heavily. "How many arsonists are current or former firefighters?"

Colin whistled softly. "Roughly thirty-five percent."

"Exactly. You need to know, I recently fired one of my captains, Jayson Sanders."

It was Colin's turn to be surprised. "You did? When?"

"Yesterday." Dorian scowled. "I hadn't made the announcement yet, so this isn't well known, but I will tell you Jay was extremely upset with me. Told me I'd regret my actions as he stormed out of my office."

"Do you mind if I ask why you terminated him?"

"There were claims of sexual harassment from the two female firefighters working for him." The chief's gaze was grim. "I questioned both women, and while most of the harassment was verbal, he'd groped Julie a couple of times. That behavior is unacceptable. And I told him as much."

"I agree." It made Colin angry to think about what the female firefighters had suffered.

"It's not a stretch to think that Jay would seek revenge against my daughter for my actions," Dorian said, his brow furrowed with anger. "Especially since I may have mentioned if those female firefighters were either of my daughters, he'd be sitting behind bars."

No, that was not a stretch. Colin was glad to have a lead, but as he texted Mitch Callahan, he silently prayed they'd find Jayson Sanders before he struck out against Faye again.

CHAPTER THREE

Faye woke to the bright sunlight beaming through a crack in the curtains that just happened to be shining directly in her face. Swallowing a groan, she rolled to the side and blinked at the clock on the nightstand, trying to see. She'd slept for three hours, which was longer than she'd expected.

But not long enough to feel refreshed and energized.

Rolling back, she threw her arm over her face, debating whether she should get up to close the drapes tighter to get more sleep. As much as her body needed the rest, her mind immediately went back to the fires in her car, and her house.

It was still difficult to believe her house was gone. Likely very little would be salvageable. And she still needed to contact her insurance company. She didn't doubt they'd drop her faster than a hot potato after paying these two claims.

And she needed to talk to her father too.

That thought had her staring up at the ceiling. Yep, it was no use. She wasn't getting any more sleep. Dragging herself out of bed, she stumbled toward the bathroom.

Colin had told her to make herself at home, so she decided to take a quick shower.

Too bad she didn't have fresh clothes to change into. Her scrubs would have to suffice.

Feeling slightly better, she made her way down to the first floor. It was so quiet she wondered if she was alone in the house. Then her gaze landed on Colin who sat in a small alcove off the main living space.

"Hey, I didn't expect you to get up so soon." His sharp gaze didn't seem to miss a thing. "If you need to change into something else, we can see what might fit you from Elly's closet."

"No, it's fine." She was self-conscious of the fact that she sported more curves than Elly, at least from what she remembered. "I was just about to call my dad."

"He stopped by while you were sleeping." Colin stood and came over to stand beside her. "Does the name Jayson Sanders mean anything to you?"

She frowned. "No, should it?"

"He's our main suspect, right behind your ex-husband." Colin took her hand and led her to the computer. "Take a look, see what you think."

Her dad had been there? They had a suspect? She'd only slept three hours but apparently had missed a lot. She sat behind the computer, looking at the firefighter's face on the screen. He wore his full dress uniform, and of course, he gazed unsmiling at the camera. Her father's picture was much the same, so that part wasn't surprising.

"I've never met him." She glanced up at Colin. "Why is he a suspect? Firefighters put out fires, they don't start them."

"Not necessarily true, you'd be surprised at how many firefighters turn arsonists. Mostly so they can play the hero running in to put the fire out, but some just like to watch things go up in flames. Or are simply fascinated with fire." He gestured to the image. "He's a suspect because your father fired him yesterday for sexual harassment."

She arched a brow. "Okay, I can see why he'd be upset with my dad. Seems like a flimsy reason to come after me. He can't be the first guy to get fired for something like that."

"Your dad specifically said he'd be tossed in jail if he'd have done anything like that to his daughters." Colin held her gaze. "Trust me, he could be lashing out at you to get back at your dad."

When he put it that way, it made more sense. She looked back at the man on the screen. "I don't know, Colin. He's big and broad across the shoulders. The person on the video didn't appear to have that same build."

"He could have changed, and the video may be deceiving. The image isn't as clear as we'd have liked. Either way, Mitch Callahan is heading over to have a little chat with him."

"That's good." She realized that if this Jayson Sanders guy was the one who set the fire, this entire mess would be over relatively quickly.

Except from the insurance company's perspective.

"I need to make some calls." Since she was sitting behind the desk, she used the computer to bring up her insurance company's website.

"Would you like some coffee?" Colin asked as she punched the numbers to their claims line into her phone.

"Sure, that would be great." She may as well have some, she'd be up now for the rest of the day.

The insurance agent who answered her call was nice enough, despite the fact that she would be costing them a significant amount of money. They promised to send an adjuster to both scenes and would be back in touch.

"What I need to do is find long-term housing." She looked up as Colin returned with her coffee. She'd heard the coffee maker brewing, so it was clearly a fresh pot.

"I think you should wait on that." Colin gestured for her to join him in the living room. "We don't know that Sanders is guilty or that Mitch has him in custody."

"I can't stay here, Colin." She tried to smile. "Your family is wonderful, but I can't impose on Devon in her condition."

"I'll stick around, too, to help out." Colin leveled her a stern look. "You can't risk being found somewhere new, Faye. Not while this guy is on the loose."

She narrowed her gaze. "Are you asking or telling?"

"Telling. Because if you did go somewhere else, and this guy finds you and ends up hurting innocent people, you'll feel responsible."

She scowled because he was right. "You're pushing it, Finnegan."

"Yeah? Sue me. I only care about keeping you safe."

Rolling her eyes at his attitude, she sipped her coffee. The caffeine wasn't working as quickly as she needed it to. "I can't just sit here all day."

"You were supposed to be sleeping." Colin paused, then reluctantly added, "Your father made it clear you're welcome to stay with him."

She wrinkled her nose before she could catch herself. A flash of mirth crossed Colin's features as she quickly added, "That's very nice of him, but I'd rather not."

"I thought you got along with your stepmother and half sister?"

"I do, but that's mostly because we don't live together.

Once I left for college, I never moved back home. I was only there for a couple of holiday breaks, but even those visits were only a day or two." She shrugged. "I'm happy for them, really. But I think my being there cramps Claire's style."

"We would really like you to stay here, then." Colin's tone was low and gentle. She didn't doubt the offer was genuine. "At least until we know this guy has been arrested."

"And what if that takes more than a day or two?" She couldn't help feeling like an interloper. Especially since she didn't have her usual twelve-hour shifts to keep her busy.

Before Colin could respond, his phone rang. She was grateful he put the call on speaker for her benefit. "Hey, Mitch. Tell me you have good news."

"I wish I could, but Sanders is in the wind." Mitch sounded disgruntled. "No one is home, and the one neighbor I was able to talk to said he hasn't seen him since yesterday when he headed off to work. Apparently, the guy across the street leaves at roughly the same time each morning, and they make a point of making sure they aren't backing their cars out of their respective driveways at the same time."

"Have you spoken to his family? He could be staying with one of them."

"I'm working on that. His ex-wife, Sadie, hasn't seen him. Sounds like he wouldn't be welcome there even if he wanted to stop by."

No surprise there. She met Colin's gaze, knowing he was thinking the same thing. Guys who sexually harassed women who worked for them weren't likely to be great husband material.

Her ex hadn't done that specifically, but she wouldn't have put such behavior past Rory either. Rory had gotten through life on his good looks, something she should have figured out before marrying him.

"What about Faye's ex-husband?" Colin asked.

"He wasn't home either. I left a message with the bar where he works as a bartender. I'm hoping he gets back to me soon."

Two dead ends, she thought grimly. Finding the arsonist was not going to be as easy as she'd hoped. She leaned forward to talk into the speaker.

"Mitch? It's Faye. My insurance company will need a copy of your reports on the two fires as soon as you have them finished."

"Hi, Faye, that's not a problem. I hope to have them completed by Monday. I still need time to thoroughly investigate your house. The scene is too hot for me to do that now."

"I understand," she quickly assured him. "Thanks for your help."

"Yes, keep us updated on your progress," Colin added.

"Will do." Mitch disconnected from the call.

They sat in silence for a moment. "How is Larry doing?" She mentally kicked herself for not asking sooner. "Should I call the hospital to see what I can find out?"

"No need." Colin's expression was somber. "He didn't make it."

"What?" She stared in horror. "Are you sure?"

"Yes, I'm sure." Colin abruptly stood and headed into the kitchen. Numb from shock and horror, she sat there, thinking of the young man.

What if that had been Colin lying there? A shiver snaked down her spine.

She bowed her head, feeling overwhelmed with despair. No matter how much she tried to convince herself otherwise, she knew the blame for Larry's death rested on her shoulders.

Hers—and if Jayson Sanders was responsible, her father's.

COLIN TOOK a moment to wrestle his emotions under control. Losing Larry had been rough. Their squad, the entire city, really, hadn't suffered a firefighter job-related death in years. Not during his time on the job, and that was almost eight years.

Sure, they all knew and accepted the risks. But in truth, they were also well trained and experts at fighting fires and taking precautions. Fire response–related deaths were rare, far less likely than police officer deaths on the job.

And they hit especially hard when they happened close to home.

He stared blindly out the front window at the quiet neighborhood. It hurt to think of Larry losing his life, but he knew it wasn't Faye's fault. No matter how much she would wallow in guilt over the loss.

Blowing out a long sigh, he hoped Mitch would find the arsonist and make him pay for what he did. Arson was a felony, and a death related to an arson event could be deemed a murder.

If Sanders or Owen were responsible, he knew they'd rot in prison for the rest of their lives.

The thought eased some of his tension. He watched as a group of young kids rode their bikes past their house, likely heading to Brookland Park. Schools wouldn't start until after September 1, and he found himself smiling a bit at the memories of how he and his siblings used to run around the neighborhood. Back when their parents were still alive.

They'd run into Faye on occasion, but she was usually sitting beneath the shade of a tree with her head in a book.

As if his mind had conjured her up, she came up to stand beside him. "I'm really sorry about Larry."

"Thanks." He moved over and gestured to the kids outside. "Brings back memories, doesn't it?"

"I was never as athletically inclined as you Finnegans." She smiled at the kids who made circles in the road before continuing on their way. "But this was a great place to grow up."

"We were very blessed." He frowned. "Even though we lost our parents, and you lost your mother, we always knew we were loved. And safe."

"Yes, we did." She sighed as if wishing for those days to return, then moved away. "Where are Rhy and Devon?"

"Buying baby furniture for their new nursery." He grinned, thinking of how perfect it was that Rhy and Devon would start a new generation of Finnegans in the homestead. "They'll probably stop for lunch along the way. If you're hungry, I can pull something together. Devon keeps the fridge well stocked."

"I'm not hungry." She glanced around the kitchen. "I really would rather head outside for a while. I can't see sitting around here all day."

Colin frowned but could see her point. If the situation was reversed, and he was staying at her father's place, he'd be itching to get out too. "Okay, it should be safe enough to head down to the park."

"Really?" Her expression brightened. "I'd like that."

"I think we have a couple of bicycles in the garage."

"Are you serious?" She paled. "I, uh, haven't been on a bike in years."

"Come on, it will be fun." He guided her toward the garage door. He took a moment to disarm the security system. "Trust me, we don't have to break any speed records. A simple casual ride to the park, okay?"

"Okay." Faye did not look convinced but readily followed him to the garage.

After reengaging the alarm, he opened the garage door and went over to where there were three bicycles standing together in the back corner. They were relatively clean, as if they'd been used recently. He checked the tires and the brakes, then wheeled them outside.

"I don't know about this," Faye muttered as she threw her leg over the seat. "I'll probably fall on my face or break my arm."

"You won't." At least, he hoped not. "Slow and steady, remember?"

She pushed off and rode down the driveway, wobbling a bit before finding her balance. He himself hadn't ridden a bike in a long time but easily caught up to her.

"Don't get too close," she warned. "I'm liable to hit you."

"You won't," he said again, but moved over to give her more room.

The August sun was already beating down on them. The park wasn't far, just over a mile, but when they arrived, Faye quickly dismounted and walked with her bike. Colin did the same, eyeing her scrubs. "We should have raided Elly's closet. You must be hot in those long scrub pants."

"No, I'm fine." She looked flushed, her cheeks pink from the sun or the exertion. Or both. She shook her head. "Besides, Elly's clothes would never fit me. I just want to walk a while so I don't make a fool of myself."

"No chance of that. You're the smartest woman I know."

That made her laugh. "Yeah, that's just a nice way of saying I was a science geek in high school."

"A smart and pretty geek," he corrected. "Intimidating to the rest of us dumb guys."

"Yeah, right." She snorted. "I remember how popular the Finnegans were. And I know you weren't dumb either."

"Not smart like you, though." He was glad to see she was relaxing as they talked. Getting out in the fresh air was a good thing. "You were the only one to graduate early and start college with credits under your belt from all your AP courses."

"I was rather single-minded in my quest to become a physician," she admitted. "When my mom died of a brain aneurysm when I was ten, I knew I wanted to be a doctor in the emergency department. I toyed briefly with being a fire-fighter, but that didn't last long. Being a doctor called to me."

"Mission accomplished." He strove to keep his tone light. "I know losing your mom must have been difficult for you."

"It was all very sudden. Much like what you and your family suffered."

They fell silent for several minutes as they strolled along the park pathway wheeling their bikes. When they reached a park bench beneath a tree, he stopped and propped his bike against the trunk, then took hers to do the same. "On the bright side, we all survived and thrived."

"We did." She sat on the bench. "How did you know this was my favorite spot?"

"I remember how you enjoyed sitting here, reading a

book." He dropped down beside her. "Although I think those were romance novels, not science books."

She chuckled and leaned back to look up at the green leaves overhead. "They were. Too bad my marriage did not work out the same way."

"What happened?"

She shook her head. "Same old story. He cheated with his yoga instructor. Tried to blame me because I worked long hours. Not that Rory didn't enjoy spending my money, because he certainly did."

"Scumbag."

That made her laugh again. It occurred to Colin that she hadn't laughed like this back in high school that he could remember. Then again, they'd been friendly acquaintances but not especially close. "Yeah, he was. But he's not my problem anymore."

"Unless he's the one behind the fires."

"Maybe. But I still can't see Rory doing that kind of thing. Wouldn't someone have to investigate how to start a fire in a way that they didn't risk being burned?"

"Yes, that would be a key component to being an arsonist," he said in a dry tone. "Which is why thirty-five percent of arsonists are either current or former firefighters."

"Rory wouldn't bother to do that much work. Ambition wasn't his strong suit." She shrugged. "Hopefully, Mitch finds that guy my father fired very soon."

"He will. Mitch is not happy about either of these fires targeting you. His wife, Dana, works in the ER, or rather the ED. It makes him especially mad when healthcare providers are in harm's way."

"I know Dana and your sister Alanna very well. They're both excellent nurses." She nodded thoughtfully. "I'm sure he won't stop until he finds the person responsible."

"Let me know when you want to head back for lunch." He grinned. "I can grill a couple of burgers if you're interested."

"That sounds nice." She glanced over to the restrooms located roughly fifty yards away. "If you don't mind, I'm going to use the restroom before we head back."

"No problem. I'll stay here to watch our bikes." There was a chain lock wrapped around the seat of one of them, but he couldn't remember the combination.

His phone rang again. Not Mitch, but his brother Rhy. "Hey, what's up?"

"Where are you and Faye?" Rhy asked. "We were worried when we saw your car was still here."

"You know we're both adults, right?" He couldn't help teasing his oldest brother.

"You know the rule is to leave a note on the white board," Rhy shot back. "It's the only way to keep track of what's going on around here."

"Okay, okay. Sorry about that." He knew his brother was a bit of a control freak, which was laughable considering nine kids coming and going was the antithesis of being in control. The homestead often resembled Grand Central station. "Honestly, I didn't expect you and Devon until later this afternoon, figured you stop for a bite to eat. Faye and I rode your bikes to Brookland Park. We'll be back shortly."

"I should have noticed the bikes were gone," Rhy groused. "Did you get any updates on the arson investigation?"

"Not yet." He filled Rhy in on the new suspect in the case. "Callahan said he wasn't home, and the neighbors haven't seen him."

"Maybe he knows Callahan is on to him."

"That's possible. He must know we'd talk to Chief

Kimble about the threat against his daughter." He watched as Faye disappeared inside the restrooms. "Did you and Devon buy out the store?"

"Pretty much. The furniture will be delivered early next week. By the way, I could use your help in painting the nursery."

"Sure." He injected enthusiasm he didn't feel into his tone. He didn't mind pitching in to help the family, but he was not fond of painting. Yet he also knew that summer was Quinn's busiest time as the Coast Guard patrolled the Great Lakes region. And Aiden was often shipped out for deployments with the National Guard. Tarin and Brady were both married and busy with their respective wives and careers, which meant he was the one with the easiest schedule to manage. "We'll coordinate on my next couple of days off."

"Thanks, Colin. We appreciate your help. Now that I know you and Faye are fine, I will take my lovely wife out to lunch as you suggested. Later, bro."

"Later, Rhy." He frowned when he noticed a figure in black moving away from the restroom structure. Was it his imagination or did that individual resemble the guy on the video taken in the parking garage?

Ditching the bikes was asking for trouble, but Colin didn't hesitate to break into a jog heading toward the spot where he'd seen the figure. The person in black had ducked through the trees, which in and of itself wasn't suspicious. Yet he couldn't deny the sense of urgency he felt in needing to get a better look at the guy.

He quickened his pace, determined to get closer. The trees around the restrooms weren't that thick, there was more parkland on the other side. If memory served, there was also a small parking lot back there. When he reached the area, he could see there was a path through the woods, no doubt worn through the grass by numerous parkgoers taking a shortcut to get to the restrooms.

Hearing a motor, he broke into a run. No! He couldn't let this guy slip away!

He broke through the line of trees, raking his gaze over the area. In the distance, he saw the figure on a motor scooter, helmet covering his head. The motor scooter had been parked in a corner of the small parking lot, away from other vehicles. Even as Colin ran toward the guy, the motor scooter backed up, then quickly turned and headed toward the road that would take him out of the park. The driver wasn't going fast, that type of scooter maxed out at thirty miles per hour.

Colin put on another burst of speed, desperate to get the license plate number. He thought he saw the number 4 and the letter M. Or maybe it was the letter A and the letter M. There wasn't enough time to get all the digits, the motor scooter turned and put on speed, leaving him with nothing but a blur. The speed limit in the park was only ten miles per hour, but that didn't stop the motor bike rider from leaving Colin in the dust.

The way the rider took off convinced Colin this was the same guy. He stopped and quickly fired off a text message to Mitch, asking him to run a motor scooter plate with the letters A and M, and the number 4 and M. Either one might be enough to get a hit on their suspect.

He hoped.

That done, he turned to head back to the restrooms. A horrible thought hit hard. He hadn't seen the guy leaving the structure, but what if he had gone inside?

Once again, he broke into a run. "Faye!" he shouted as he approached the trees. "Faye, are you in there?"

There was nothing but silence.

The scent of burning wood wafted toward him. As he ducked through the trees along the path, he saw dark smoke billowing from the building.

The arsonist had started the restrooms on fire!

CHAPTER FOUR

Faye had been washing her hands at the sink when a strange scent tickled her nose. She frowned, trying to place it. Cleaning solution? No, acetone. She remembered using it to clean her brushes after staining the baseboards of her bedroom. Reaching for paper towels, she glanced over her shoulder wondering if the acetone was being used in the park for some reason. Why, she couldn't fathom.

The scent grew stronger, sending a frisson of unease down her spine. She reached for the door, then snatched her hand back when the handle was hot to the touch.

Hot? Fear morphed into panic. She couldn't see the flames but knew the door to the women's restroom was on fire.

"Colin!" She backed away from the door, coughing a bit as smoke began to fill the enclosed space. "Colin! Can you hear me?"

No answer.

Swallowing hard, she told herself to stay calm. There had to be a way out. Looking up, she saw a small vent along the outside wall. It was positioned in the corner, the upper frame about an inch from the ceiling.

Out of her reach, but that didn't stop her from approaching the sink. She pressed hard on the ceramic, wondering if it would hold her weight. She was no slim Jim, but maybe it would hold her long enough to get the vent off?

There was only one way to find out.

More smoke seeped in beneath the door, bringing a haze that stung her eyes and caused more coughing. She was all too aware of the danger, having treated many patients with smoke inhalation during her career. Turning on the faucet in the sink, she tore off her scrub top and pushed the fabric into the water. Wringing it out, she put the top on backward so that the V was in the back. This way, she could pull the fabric up over her mouth and nose. Breathing through the damp cloth made her feel better.

Still, it wouldn't work for long. She needed to get out of there!

Lifting her leg, she placed her knee on the edge of the sink, then pushed upward, placing her hands against the wall. Thankfully, the wall to her left wasn't hot to the touch, or she'd be in trouble. Balancing there for a moment, she pulled her other leg up to kneel on the sink.

So far, so good.

Reaching up to the grate, she groaned when she realized she was an inch short. Shifting a bit for a better angle, she tried again. This time her fingertips brushed the bottom edge of the grate.

It wasn't enough!

Stifling a sob, she did her best to bring her foot up to the edge of the sink. Was it her imagination, or did the sink pull away from the wall a bit?

Don't think about that. Just get yourself up to the grate!

Sweat ran down the sides of her face from exertion. She wasn't graceful or athletic, and she expected to fall on her face at any moment. Someone in the park must have seen the fire by now and called 911, but so far, she didn't hear any sirens.

Come on, you can do this!

Somehow, she was able to lever herself high enough to get her second foot up on the sink. Bracing one hand against the wall for balance, she pushed on the grate with the other.

It didn't move, not even a quarter inch.

"Colin!" She pulled the fabric down from her mouth so she could be heard. "Colin!"

"Faye! I'm here. The fire crew is on the way."

The news was only slightly reassuring. She pulled the fabric up again over her nose and mouth and beat on the grate with her fist. Did it move? She hit it again and again, hoping and praying she'd manage to knock it loose.

How she'd get through the opening was another obstacle, but one she didn't dwell on. The good news about being up this high was that a hint of fresh air wafted through the narrow opening.

"Faye!" The grate moved beneath her fingertips. Then it was gone, and she saw Colin's concerned face in the opening. "I'm here. Are you hurt?"

"No." She blinked away tears, struggling to remain calm. Normally she was cool under pressure, at least as far as working with a slew of patients coming through the emergency department.

This type of thing was beyond her normal coping skills.

"Can you push up any higher? Crawl through the opening?" Colin's gaze held hers. "I'm here to support you on this side."

It seemed an impossible task. Yet she'd managed to get

this far. Glancing down, she placed one foot on the top of the faucet and pushed upward. Her face was through the opening now, but she knew there was no way on earth she'd get the rest of body through.

Stupid tears filled her eyes again. So close! She was so close to getting out of the smoky bathroom. Hearing the wail of sirens brought some relief. Help was on the way.

The sink beneath her feet abruptly broke away from the wall. She let out a yelp and managed to grab onto the lower part of the opening where the grate had been to keep from hitting the floor.

"Faye!" Colin covered her hands with his. "Are you okay?"

She didn't have the breath to answer. Craning her neck, she peered down to see where the sink was, knowing she wouldn't be able to hold herself there for long. She'd never managed to do a pull-up in her entire life. Doubtful she'd be able to do one now.

"Can you hang on a little longer?" Colin looked down at her through the grate opening.

"I don't know." Her voice was muffled against the wall. If she let go, she'd land on the broken remains of the sink. Telling herself it could be worse, she struggled to remain calm. "Just hurry."

"I won't leave you." His low voice was husky.

"I know." Turning her head from the wall, she coughed. The bathroom door was dark with soot. Or was it blackened wood? An orange flame licked through a narrow opening in the doorway. She watched in horror as the flicker grew longer, as if it were a long, fiery finger reaching toward her.

How long before the door was completely engulfed in flames?

Her fingers cramped on the edge of the grate opening.

She wasn't going to be able to hold herself much longer. The sirens were loud now, so much so that she could no longer hear Colin's reassuring voice.

Her fingers slipped. Placing one foot against the wall, she pushed her body away and let go. She hit the floor hard, narrowly missing the largest chunk of the broken sink.

Stumbling back, she put as much distance between herself and the burning door. The smoke was thicker now and getting worse by the second.

Then she heard a sizzle as water pummeled the door. A few droplets made it through the cracks, but not enough to help alleviate the smoke. If anything, the smoke thickened.

Faye dropped to the floor in the furthest corner of the room, burying her face in the wet fabric of her scrub top.

Her eyes burned, tears streaking down her cheeks. Deep voices from the other side of the door brought hope of rescue.

Finally, a section of the door gave way, water pouring through the opening. She struggled to her feet, although getting soaked was the least of her concerns. She wanted desperately to escape, to rush through the opening into the fresh air, but held back. The fire might be under control, but that didn't mean it was safe. Whatever part of the door was left would be sizzling hot.

A fireman burst through the opening. "Faye?"

"Here." Her voice was a croak.

He stepped forward, compassion in his gaze through his face mask. "I'm going to cover you with this blanket to get you out, okay?"

"Yes." She nodded in case he couldn't hear her. Without hesitation, he tossed the blanket over her head, then placed his arm around her waist, guiding her across the room and through the opening.

She walked with him for several feet before she heard Colin's voice. "Thanks, Darrel. I can take it from here." The blanket came off. She blinked, realizing she was standing near an ambulance.

"I'm going to place this oxygen mask over your face, okay?" A kind paramedic tugged the scrub top away to place a face mask over her nose and mouth. She thought about protesting but understood the medical treatment was appropriate and necessary. She needed to be a good patient and let these first responders do their job.

Despite the oxygen, she coughed and coughed, her lungs desperately trying to eliminate the smoke irritant. Her vision was still blurry, but she focused on Colin's grim features hovering over her. It took a minute for her to register the fact that the paramedics had gently pushed her down onto a stretcher.

Her arm shot out to grab Colin. "Don't take me to the hospital."

"You need to get checked out." He hunkered down beside her. "If our situation was reversed, and I was the one lying there, you'd make me go in."

Yeah, she would, but this was different. "I just need to rest for a few minutes." She coughed again, then added, "Oxygen is helping."

"I'm sure it is." He took her hands, scowling at the abrasions on her palms. He took a cleansing wipe and softly removed the bits of debris. He applied antibiotic ointment and loosely wrapped them in gauze. His thoughtful concern choked her up. Never in their short marriage had Rory been so sweet and kind.

She took in a deep breath, pulling herself together with an effort. She wasn't hurt badly, at least from a physical perspective. Her lungs would heal in time. Emotionally, the fear of burning to death hadn't faded.

"Did you see who did this?" She sounded as if she'd smoked an entire carton of cigarettes. And her throat felt like it too.

"A figure in black took off on a motor scooter." Colin shook his head. "I only caught a partial plate and asked Mitch to run it for us. I haven't heard back yet."

"How?" She caught his hand. "How were we found?"

"I don't know, Faye." His gaze was troubled. "Maybe we were followed to the homestead. Maybe our alarm system was enough to keep them from attempting to breach the house."

Horrifying to imagine the damage that could have been done to the Finnegan homestead, or worse, to its occupants. She closed her eyes on a wave of despair.

She needed to find someplace to stay. Not at her father's house, or with the Finnegans. Not now.

No one was safe around her. *No one.*

COLIN'S RELIEF over getting Faye out of danger was short-lived. Her questions were dead-on. He wasn't a cop like his siblings, but he'd watched for a tail.

Obviously, he hadn't done a good enough job of evading the arsonist. And really, looking back, he should have taken more time at the scene of her house fire. He knew full well many firebugs liked to stay close to watch their handiwork. It was all part of the fascination with the dancing dragon, the term many used to describe fire.

The close call with Faye had brought him to his knees.

He'd mistakenly assumed the arsonist had just wanted to make things difficult for her.

Now he knew the ultimate goal was to kill her. Not with a bullet, but with fire.

"We should take her to the ER," the paramedic said in a low voice.

"ED," he absently corrected. "We can try, but she made it clear she doesn't want to go."

"I'm fine." Faye's voice was stronger now, and her coughing had subsided a bit. "Please give me a few more minutes."

"You'll need to sign a waiver if you refuse to be transported to the hospital," the paramedic warned.

"That's fine. The only treatment for smoke inhalation is oxygen. I didn't breathe in enough smoke to need anything more complex, like hyperbaric treatments."

Colin raised a brow. "Hyperbaric treatments?" That was knowledge outside his paramedic training. "What does that entail?"

She waved a gauzy hand. "Never mind. It's complicated. Just know I'm not that bad, I'll recover without a problem. Thankfully, being near the grate opening helped. And I covered my nose and mouth too."

He tended to agree with her assessment. He'd rescued victims who had looked far worse. Hard to argue with her medical knowledge, too, although he knew full well that doctors and nurses made the worst patients.

"Fine with me." The paramedic shrugged and tapped on a computer tablet. Everything was computerized these days, so he pulled up the form electronically and thrust the tablet toward her. "Sign here."

Faye sat up on the gurney to take it. She blinked, her eyes red and irritated, and used the tip of her finger to sign.

Then she removed the face mask and looked at him. "I'm ready to go."

"Okay. But Mitch Callahan just arrived. He'll want to talk to you first."

She nodded and put the face mask back over her nose and mouth for a few more deep breaths as the arson investigator approached.

"Colin, what happened?" Mitch looked from him to Faye. "I don't like this turn of events."

"Me either." Faye set the face mask aside.

Colin filled Mitch in on what he saw first, then handed the thread to Faye. Her comments were concise and brief, void of any emotion. It was as if she were describing an event that had happened to someone else.

"I got several hits on the motor scooter license plate, but it will take time to go through them all." Mitch shook his head. "I was surprised by how many scooters we have registered in the state."

"Maybe we can narrow them to the Milwaukee area?" Colin suggested.

"I don't think that's wise," Mitch said. "We don't know for sure who this guy is. He could have bought and registered the motor scooter in another city and moved here more recently."

"I take it Rory Owen and Jayson Sanders aren't on the list?"

"That's correct. They are not." Mitch shifted his gaze back to Faye. "I think it's time for you to tell us which patients and families may be upset with you."

She grimaced. "I really can't."

"I've initiated a subpoena requesting records from Trinity Medical Center on patient complaints lodged against you personally over the past year." Mitch spread his hands. "I'll find out eventually. You can help by giving me a place to start."

She shook her head. "When you have the list, we'll go through it. But I can't do anything until you have that subpoena."

Colin saw the frustration in Mitch's eyes, but he didn't say anything more. Faye wasn't going to breach patient confidentiality, and that was that.

As annoying as it was, he had to admire her resolve.

"Okay, I need to see what accelerant the guy used this time." Mitch turned to look at the blackened remnants of the restroom door.

"Acetone," Faye said.

Colin glanced at her in surprise. "How do you know?"

"I caught the scent before I realized the door was on fire." She coughed, then added, "I was washing my hands. By the time I dried them and reached for the door handle, it was hot to the touch."

"When I came around to the door, the fire was already spreading." Colin swallowed against the panic he'd felt at knowing Faye was trapped inside. "I think there was some paper or something stuck between the narrow opening right near the door handle."

"That makes sense." Mitch nodded at Faye. "Please keep in touch, Dr. Kimble. I really need your help to find this guy."

"Please call me Faye. And I'll help in any way I can. Within legal bounds," she added.

Colin watched as Mitch walked toward the scene, torn between joining him to examine the door more closely and sticking close to Faye.

Not much of a contest, he wouldn't leave Faye, even for

a minute. Look what had happened in the short time she'd been away from him here at the park?

His bright idea to take a bike ride had backfired in a big way. He frowned. "Would you rather take a rideshare back to the homestead?"

"No need." She glanced around as if remembering the bikes at the last minute. "Unless the bikes were stolen?"

"I don't think so, but I'll have to check." Worrying about the bikes hadn't been on his list of priorities. He'd pulled the picnic table over to the restrooms to get to the grate, but the stupid opening hadn't been large enough to get through. He'd grabbed a branch and tried to break through to make a larger opening, but to no avail.

By then the fire rigs had arrived, so he'd abandoned that idea. He'd wanted to be the one to go in to get Faye, but that wasn't an option without the proper gear. Especially since the wood remains of the door were still smoldering when Darrel had agreed to go in to get her. They'd doused the fire, but it took time for the heat to dissipate.

Faye set the oxygen mask aside and stood. "I'm ready."

Cupping her elbow in his hand, he guided her toward the park bench where they'd stopped to rest—he glanced at his watch—only forty minutes ago.

It seemed like a lifetime. More so for Faye, though, as she'd been the one trapped by the blaze.

Thankfully, their bikes were exactly where he'd left them. Yet watching Faye place her bandaged hands on the handlebar, he changed his mind.

"Hold on." He put a hand on her arm. "We'll call Rhy. His SUV is large enough to stick the bikes in the back."

"No!" Faye's eyes widened in panic. "We're not dragging your brother and his wife into this. I can't bear the idea of this guy striking out at your family. We'll ride these back, and then you'll drop me off at the nearest hotel." She held his gaze. "We're not even going inside, understand?"

He wanted to argue, but she had a point about putting his family in danger. "We'll ride back," he reluctantly agreed. "And then I'll take you someplace safe."

"Good." She let out a sigh and nodded. "That's good."

He wasn't leaving her alone, but that was an argument for later. Right now, it was more important to get back to his Jeep.

Mitch came over before they could get on the bikes. "Need a lift?"

"Are you finished here?" Colin asked in surprise. He figured Mitch would have stuck around for a while.

"I have what I need for now." He gestured to his SUV. "Let me give you a ride home."

"Thanks." Faye appeared relieved not to have to ride the bike.

It took longer to get the bikes stored in the back than it did for Mitch to drive them back to the homestead. Mitch helped pull the bikes out as Colin punched in the key code to open the garage door.

The alarm was only for the house, and when the garage door opened, he was relieved to see the empty space where Rhy's SUV would normally be. That's right, he'd mentioned taking Devon out for lunch. A good thing as he wouldn't have to stop to fill his oldest brother in on the recent events at the park.

After storing the bikes in the corner where he'd found them, Colin closed the garage door and used his key to unlock the Jeep.

"Stay in touch," Mitch said, giving Faye a stern look as she climbed into the passenger-side seat.

"I promise." She smiled wearily before closing the door.

"Keep me in the loop on what you find out," Colin said. He waited for Mitch to nod, then slid in behind the wheel.

Mitch backed out of the driveway first. Then Colin did the same, feeling a twinge of regret at the need to leave the homestead. He made a mental note to call Rhy later as he drove through their Brookland neighborhood.

"There's a hotel near the hospital," Faye said, breaking the silence. "It's within walking distance, and there's a shuttle service as many patients' families stay there. That will work the best for me. I have to report back to work on Monday."

"I don't think that's a good idea. The arsonist might figure out that's where you're staying."

"It's a big place, even if he thinks I'm there, there's no way he can figure out which room I'm in."

Colin shook his head. "You really want to put others at risk?"

"No! But so far this guy has only targeted me, Colin. There was no one else in the restroom with me, and he only hit my house and my car." She sounded frustrated, and while he could relate, he wasn't buying her theory.

"Larry was killed fighting the fire at your house, so he clearly doesn't care how many other innocent lives he takes down with him."

She sucked in a harsh breath, then coughed. "Just leave me downtown, then," she said in a low voice. "I'll stay somewhere else. No one but me will know where I am."

"I can't do that." The thought of her being completely on her own was unacceptable. No way, not happening. He didn't care what she said, he wasn't leaving her to navigate the danger on her own. "I'm staying with you."

"No, you're not." Her jaw jutted stubbornly. "Anyone staying near me is in danger. I'm not shouldering the burden for your safety too." She sighed, and added, "Please don't ask me to do that."

He tried to find the words to reassure her. "Faye, we need to leave our worries in God's hands. My decision to stay with you is my choice. I believe God will watch over us."

She didn't say anything for a long moment. He considered heading to the American Lodge but decided against it. If the arsonist was a former firefighter, he'd know to look for them there. Gary, the owner, was a former firefighter himself and offered a discount for police and fire responders.

"Please don't ask me to leave you, because I can't do that. If I hadn't been at the park with you today . . ." He let his voice trail off.

"I don't want you to be hurt because of me." Her voice was low and husky.

"I feel the exact same way." He took her hand in his. "I wouldn't be able to live with myself if something happened to you because I wasn't there to help protect you."

She didn't say anything for a long time.

"Don't you see? We're better off sticking together." He headed downtown, away from Brookland and Trinity Medical Center.

"Okay, we can stay together, for now." She sounded so exhausted and worn out that he didn't take any joy in getting his way.

Now all he needed to do was keep her safe. Hopefully, it wouldn't take Mitch too long to find this guy, getting him off the street once and for all.

CHAPTER FIVE

Allowing Colin to stay close was a mistake. Logically, she knew that. Practically, it was difficult to say no. For one thing she didn't have a car or a place to stay. She also didn't own anything but what she had in her purse and the scrubs she wore. Dirty, wet, stained scrubs that she couldn't wait to get rid of.

She made a silent promise to convince Colin to leave after they'd stopped to get new clothes and decided on temporary housing. The idea of a hotel didn't thrill her, but without a vehicle to get groceries, she didn't have another option. Unless they were able to find a vacation rental close to a grocery store.

"I'd like to stop and get a few things." She plucked at the scrubs. "Real clothes would be nice. These smell like smoke."

"Sure, where do you usually shop?" He glanced at her curiously. "I can take you to the mall if that helps."

"No need. A discount store will do for now." Not smart to spend a bunch of money when she had no idea what the insurance company would do related to her car and house.

Did they pay if the loss was related to a crime? She had no idea.

"Are you sure? I don't mind."

"I'm positive. I only need a few things to get through the rest of the weekend. I'll be back at work on Monday."

Colin looked like he wanted to argue but then nodded. Using the Jeep's GPS screen, he pulled up a map. "There's a discount store about five miles from here."

"Perfect." Rubbing her temple, she tried not to dwell on how close she'd been to being burned. Or suffering extreme smoke inhalation. Both could be deadly.

Which seemed to have been the goal. Unlike the previous attempts that had simply damaged her personal property.

"It seems odd that a firefighter who'd lost his job would risk killing me." She was having trouble coming up with a viable reason why anyone would want to kill her. "Same goes for an irate patient or family member. It's so drastic. And extreme. If caught and convicted, they'd face life in prison without the possibility of parole."

"He's already killed Larry, but that may have not been intentional. Not like the fire in the restroom. I've been thinking about that too," Colin admitted. "The fire may not have been intended to harm you. Especially as it was set in the middle of the day in August when kids are still out of school and known to play at the park. I wasn't the only one to call 911, they'd already received other calls related to the fire."

She shivered, remembering those panicked moments she'd been trapped. "The arsonist may have underestimated the impact of severe smoke inhalation, then. If not for you helping to remove that grate, things could have ended with me being intubated and placed in a critical care unit." Or worse. Hyperbaric treatments were a last-ditch resort and didn't always work to reverse the impact of severely damaged lung tissue.

"I know." He took her hand. "I still wish you had gone in to be evaluated."

"I'm fine." Her throat was still sore, and her voice sounded scratchy, but her coughing had mostly subsided.

"Maybe we need to think about which patients may have died under your care." Colin pulled into the parking lot of a popular discount store. "This may be about revenge."

"I don't keep a list. Besides, we already talked about patient privacy, remember?" She pushed out of the passenger door, frustrated over the way Colin and Mitch didn't seem to understand her position.

Colin seemed just as annoyed, slamming his driver's side door harder than necessary. She scowled at him, then hurried inside. She wasn't rehashing the subject again. She would not provide names outside of a subpoena. End of discussion.

Rolling her cart through the aisles, she chose a few simple summery outfits. Ignoring Colin standing beside her, she then headed over to purchase underclothes too. Lastly, she picked up several personal items.

Colin didn't say anything until they were standing in line, waiting to check out. "I have plenty of cash if you need it."

"I don't." She wasn't taking his money, even though it was a sweet offer. Again, very different from her ex-husband. Rory expected her to pay for everything, including his incidentals. Which she'd gladly done, until she happened to see a few of his text messages with his yoga instructor. Then she'd come home early from a shift to find

Rory and Tiffany in bed together. She shook off the depressing thoughts, and added, "I'm fine, thanks."

When she'd finished paying for her things, Colin took the bag as they headed back to his Jeep. He opened her door for her. "There's a hotel near the courthouse; it seems to be reasonably priced and would be a good place to stay for a few days. Close to restaurants anyway. Give me a minute to see if they have any rooms."

She shrugged and slid into the passenger seat. "Sure, why not? I'll stay there until Monday, then I need to find a place closer to the hospital."

He frowned but didn't argue. He made the call while she listened. When he gave his name and credit card number, she put her hand on his arm and rummaged in her purse with the other. He shook his head and continued providing the information.

"We're all set." He pulled out of the parking lot and headed downtown. She didn't usually hang out down here. Her world pretty much consisted of work and being home. The area appeared busy, likely due to the summer tourist season. She was surprised the hotel had a room available over the weekend on short notice.

"I can pay my own way, Colin." She wasn't happy that he'd put the room in his name. "I'm accepting enough hospitality by you carting me around. I'd rather foot the bill for the hotel room. And why did you ask for a weeklong stay? I told you this was only for the weekend. I need to be closer to the hospital come Monday."

"We'll see how it goes." His noncommittal response irked her.

"No, Colin. I'm telling you that's what I want to do." She crossed her arms over her chest. "I can't imagine anyone will find me there."

"We didn't think anyone would find us in the park either." His tone held an edge of stubbornness.

Talking to him was beginning to feel like talking to a rock. It was taking more energy than she had to spare after being up all night and getting only three hours of sleep. The adrenaline rush she'd experienced while trapped had faded, leaving her feeling sick and worn out.

"Whatever." She hated being crabby, but it was partially his fault. She closed her eyes and strove to relax. Stress was never good for the body. Or the soul.

When the car stopped, she opened her eyes, realizing they'd arrived. Had she dozed for a few minutes? She must have. He turned in his seat to face her. "If you want to pay for the room, I won't argue, but it's a two-bedroom suite because that's all they had left. I'll gladly pay half, and I would also ask that you work with me on the best way to keep you safe. I don't want anything to happen to you."

"I'll try." She could be noncommittal too.

Colin shrugged, grabbed her bag from the store, and escorted her inside. The two-bedroom suite was on the third floor. Faye provided her credit card to pay for the room, then followed Colin to the elevator.

She unlocked the door and pushed it open, relieved to note the room was neat and clean. The only bad scent was coming from her, so she held out her hand for the bag. "I'm going to shower, change, and get some rest."

"Sounds good." Colin handed her the bag. "I'll be here when you wake up."

Oddly, she was touched by his statement. Considering she hadn't wanted him to stay, she was selfishly glad not to be alone.

Maybe she was the rock because her brain wasn't making any sense. A long shower helped ease her discomfort while also getting rid of the smell of smoke. Wearing fresh, clean clothes felt amazing.

She crawled into bed and closed her eyes. Being targeted by an arsonist was frightening, but it was her conflicted feelings for Colin that remained front and center in her mind as she drifted off to sleep.

A thudding noise woke her from a sound sleep. Fear lanced deep. She slipped out of bed, tugging the T-shirt she wore as sleepwear down, and crept to the door, listening intently.

Raucous laughter from the other side of the apparently thin wall made her relax. The sound was nothing sinister. Just other guests enjoying themselves.

Yawning, she peered at the clock. Two hours had passed. She was still exhausted but knew she couldn't sleep any longer. Getting back on a regular sleep schedule was necessary since she was scheduled for another string of four twelve-hour day shifts starting Monday.

She dressed in navy-blue capri pants and a matching green-and-blue short-sleeved blouse, ran a brush through her hair, then opened her door. She paused, hearing Colin on the phone.

"Are you sure Owen isn't involved?" Assuming he was talking to Mitch, she stepped forward to join him. He caught her gaze and smiled, his gaze lighting up with appreciation. She had to remind herself he was just being nice and willed herself not to blush. "He may have paid someone to do this."

"He wouldn't spend his money on getting back at me," she protested in a low voice.

"Hang on, Mitch, I'm putting you on speaker." He set the phone down, hit a button, then continued. "Faye is with me now."

"Hi, Mitch. I am positive Rory wouldn't spend a dime to get back at me. He'd either do something himself or do his best to ignore me altogether."

"I tend to agree with you, Faye," Mitch said. "I interviewed him for twenty minutes. Sorry to say, he came across as a self-centered jerk with nothing good to say about you. But he claims to have an alibi for the time frame of the first two fires."

"Let me guess, is her name Tiffany?" She met Colin's gaze. "Last I heard, he was seeing his yoga instructor."

"That's correct." Mitch agreed. "He said they were in an early class that started at six thirty, then went out for breakfast afterward. I'm verifying that now, but I don't think he's our guy."

"He doesn't sound smart enough to be an arsonist," Colin drawled.

"Not smart enough and not willing to get his manicured hands dirty." Mitch sighed. "I'll look into his financials, but I don't see him paying an arsonist either."

"He wouldn't waste the money." She never really considered her ex to be a viable suspect, but even less so now that she knew he had an alibi. "Money is important to Rory. So much so I'm a bit surprised he's still with Tiffany."

"I hear you. Tiffany and her business partner Alicia own two studios, but while they're doing well, they're not raking in tons of cash," Mitch said. "I spoke briefly to Tiffany as well. She hadn't even heard about the fires and seemed genuinely surprised that we suspected Owen."

"That leaves us with Jayson Sanders and the list of patient complaints against Faye," Colin said.

"It does. Still no sign of Sanders, he hasn't been home. The judge signed off on the subpoena for the patient complaints, so we're just waiting for Trinity to supply the list. I spoke to a Danielle in risk management; she promised to send it via email as soon as possible."

Since the hospital was cooperating, there wasn't anything she could do about it. At least they were covered legally to search for suspects among her patients.

"Why don't you head over once you have it?" Colin suggested.

"Will do. I'll check in with you both later."

"Thanks, Mitch." Colin reached over to end the call, still watching her. "You look well rested. Are you hungry?"

Since the hour was going on two o'clock in the afternoon, she nodded. On cue, her stomach growled with hunger. "Yes, lunch sounds good."

"There's a couple of places within walking distance." Colin stood and headed toward the door.

She snagged her purse and followed him out the door and down the elevator. As they headed outside, she hesitated. They'd assumed they were safe earlier when they'd taken a simple bike ride. What if she was found again?

"Faye?" Colin held the door for her. "Are you okay?"

"Fine." She joined him outside.

"Hey." He caught her hand in his and turned her to face him. "I know you're scared. But we can't live in fear. I know for sure we weren't followed this time. I made several turns and even backtracked before coming here. We're going to be okay."

"I know." She forced a smile she didn't feel. "Let's go."

Colin continued holding her hand as they strolled along the sidewalk. It occurred to her that she hadn't shared a meal, much less two meals, with another man since her marriage had ended.

Don't go there, she silently warned. This wasn't a date.

Far from it. Colin was a friend with an odd compulsion to protect her.

Expecting anything more was a sure path to heartache.

HOLDING hands with Faye as they strolled downtown would be even better if he didn't have to be on alert for the arsonist. Not that he expected to see the guy in black riding a motor scooter or some other form of transportation. He hadn't lied about making sure they hadn't been followed.

Despite his career choice of fighting fires, he'd learned a few cop techniques along the way. They'd come in handy while helping his brother Quinn last month. Not that he'd been able to assist Quinn and Sami as much as he'd wanted to. His brother had refused help, not wanting to put the family in danger.

After everything that had transpired so far today, Colin understood his brother's sentiment completely. While Faye had slept, he'd filled Rhy in on their current location. His brother was upset to hear about the fire. He'd assured Rhy that he and Faye would stay far away from the homestead until the arsonist was caught.

And he wasn't leaving Faye alone until that happened either. Although how they'd manage to stay close once she returned to work and he was forced to return to the fire station was yet to be determined.

The perp was likely Sanders; he held the biggest grudge against the chief. If not him, then hopefully they'd find a clue on the list of disgruntled patients. If both of those turned up with nothing, he was at a complete loss as to how to find this guy.

"I can't get over how many people are around," Faye said, breaking into his thoughts.

He cocked a brow. "Don't get out much, do you?"

"Not really." She flushed and shrugged. "Especially not downtown."

"The café is that way." He stopped at the corner, gesturing to a café a few blocks down from the courthouse. "My brother-in-law, Bax Scala, says they have good food."

"Why does that name sound familiar?" Faye asked as they waited for the light to turn green so they could cross the street.

"He was the prosecutor on a big case back in March." He gently tugged on her hand when the light changed. "The musician would have been found guilty of murder if not for my sister shooting him in the courtroom after being shot herself."

"That's right, I remember." Faye shook her head. "I was working that day. We received the trauma alert about multiple gunshot victims." Then she frowned. "Your entire family tends to run right into the line of fire, don't they?"

"Pretty much." He didn't mention how they all worried about Elly, their youngest sibling. So far, she seemed to be holding her own as an EMT, but they all expected her to change her mind at some point about the career path she'd chosen. She was so tenderhearted they feared the harsh reality of EMT work would get to her. "Much like you, Faye."

"Me?" She gaped. "Hardly."

"You run toward injured patients, which is the same thing." He remembered how quickly she'd responded to the injured firefighters.

"I guess." She didn't look convinced.

Colin half expected to see Bax, but there was no sign of

his brother-in-law at the café. Spying an empty table, he hustled over to nab it. "Sit here. I'll get our food." When she opened her mouth to argue, he held up his hand. "How about you just stop arguing for once? This is my treat. I insist."

"Me argue? That should be your middle name." Her words were tart, but she dropped into the chair, a sign of giving in.

He suppressed the urge to laugh. If she only knew how much his mother had drilled manners into them as kids, she would realize she was fighting a losing battle.

"I'll have the turkey wrap, please," she finally said. "And a water."

"Great. I'll be back soon."

It didn't take long for their sandwiches to be ready. Colin brought their meals over and took the seat across from hers. Reaching for her hand, he said, "I'd like to say grace."

"Of course." Faye bowed her head.

"Lord Jesus, we thank You for keeping us safe. Please continue to watch over us and those helping to seek justice. Amen."

"And we thank You for this food. Amen," Faye added.

Touched by her prayer, he reluctantly released her. "That was nice, thanks."

"I'm impressed by your faith, and that of your family." Faye opened her water bottle and took a sip. "I can't say I meet many people who pray like you do."

"It was always a practice in our family while growing up. I give Rhy credit for keeping the family traditions going after we lost our parents. He set a good example for us."

"My dad stopped attending church after my mother died." She toyed with her water bottle for a moment before unwrapping her sandwich. "I guess I did the same thing."

"Hey, it's okay." He smiled and reached for his sandwich. "God is always there, waiting for you."

She nodded, her expression thoughtful. They ate in silence for a few minutes, enjoying the sunshine pouring through the window. When his phone buzzed, he glanced at the text message from Mitch.

"What is it?" Faye leaned forward to see the screen, reading the message upside down. "Mitch has the list?"

"He does. He'll meet us back at the hotel in thirty minutes." He was relieved to have something tangible to work on. Being alone in the suite with Faye made him slightly uncomfortable. It was almost—too much togetherness. Not to mention too much downtime. Normally, he'd be at the gym working out, not sitting around chitchatting.

He wasn't sure why he was so hyperaware of her. Granted, she was beautiful, smart, and compassionate . . .

Well, maybe he did know. He'd always admired Faye, especially when they were in high school. She probably didn't remember that they'd had a physics class together. One he wouldn't have passed without her help on their team project.

He'd wanted to ask her to prom. Then he'd heard she was leaving school early to attend college, which put a crimp in that plan. She probably wouldn't have gone with him anyway. He couldn't remember seeing her at one of their school dances.

And why was he thinking about stuff that happened more than twelve years ago? They were both thirty years old. Well past high school drama.

She finished her meal, wrapping the garbage into a small ball. "I'm ready to go when you are."

"Okay." He wasn't in a hurry to get back to the hotel, and they had plenty of time until their meeting with Mitch, so he took his time finishing his roast beef sandwich. "Do you always eat so fast?"

She flushed and shrugged. "Job hazard. We don't get much time for meal breaks. Especially since we're often short-staffed."

"I thought my brother Rhy had logged the world's record for devouring food." He shot her a teasing smile. "You give him a run for his money."

She rolled her eyes. "Thanks, I'll make a note to slow down so I don't steal his record."

That made him laugh. "You're a good sport, Faye. You fit right in with the rest of the Finnegans." As soon as the comment left his mouth, he wished it back. "I, uh, didn't mean you'd have to keep hanging around us or anything. Just that it's nice you don't take offense."

She smiled wryly. "Thanks, I think."

He mentally smacked himself as he finished his water bottle. He stood and gathered their garbage together. "Okay, let's walk back to the hotel."

"Too bad we can't sit outside the courthouse." She lifted a hand to block the sun from her eyes. "I didn't realize there was a park area here."

"You need to get down here more often." He wanted to ask her to attend the Irish Festival down at the lakefront with him. He and his siblings attended the festival each year if they could. He didn't think there had been an Irish Fest that a Finnegan hadn't been in attendance. But their schedules made it impossible for everyone to attend at the same time.

"I do," Faye agreed. "Let's walk across the park, okay?"

"Sure." He took her hand again because he wanted to, not because he was concerned about anything going awry. "Hey, there's Bax now." He waved at his brother-in-law.

"Hi, Colin." Bax wore one of his expensive suits, not a tuxedo this time, but a nicely tailored suit that probably cost more than his weekly paycheck. "What brings you to the courthouse?"

"Bax, this is Dr. Faye Kimble. Faye, this is Kyleigh's husband, Bax. Otherwise known as Penguin."

"Nice to meet you, Dr. Kimble." Bax ignored the nickname they'd dubbed him when he'd shown up at Rhy and Devon's small wedding wearing a tux. Even the groom hadn't worn one. Much less a tuxedo that was owned, not rented.

"Please call me Faye." She elbowed Colin in the side. "Be nice."

"Hey, I'm not the one who started it."

"I don't mind," Bax said with a grin. "I've come to respect penguins. Have you seen them at the Milwaukee Zoo? They're amazing birds. And they mate for life." He pinned Colin with a look. "Something you and the rest of your family should be grateful for."

"You mean Kyleigh should be grateful," he shot back.

"No, I have a feeling if anything went wrong between us, you and your family would squash me like a bug," Bax said. Then he lowered his tone. "They're more brawn than brains, you know."

Faye laughed, a musical sound Colin wished he could hear more often. He shook his head in mock dismay. "You make it hard to tease you, brother." He noticed Bax looking at his watch. "We'll let you get back to work. Tell Kyleigh hi from me."

"Yeah, I will. Sorry, I have to meet with a witness." Bax smiled at Faye again. "Good luck with this hotshot. If he gives you any trouble, call me."

Colin moved aside so Bax could get back to work. He

watched as his brother-in-law strode quickly away. When he turned back toward Faye, a glow of fire caught the corner of his eye.

What in the world?

A flaming bottle was flying toward them. His brain registered it as a Molotov cocktail even as he threw himself at Faye. They tumbled to the ground, his body covering hers.

He felt the sear of heat as the flaming bottle flew past, missing them by a fraction of an inch.

CHAPTER SIX

Her head hit the grassy earth with a bouncing thud. Her breath tangled in her throat as Colin's heavy weight pinned her down. Smelling gasoline, Faye tried to lift her head to see what was going on. She hadn't heard gunfire, but nearby pedestrians screamed, their footsteps pounding the ground as they ran away as if there was some sort of impending threat.

"What happened?" She pushed the question through her tight throat.

"Keep your head down." Colin jumped to his feet. She didn't follow his orders but pushed herself up onto her hands and knees, her gaze fixated on a spreading fire roughly six feet away. For a moment, she was confused as to why the green grass was burning, then she remembered the gasoline scent.

Someone had chucked a firebomb at them. Granted, it was a small one, but if the gasoline had drenched her clothes and Colin's, they'd have suffered bad burns.

Colin's quick reflexes had saved their lives.

"I told you to stay down," Colin barked as he cleared the

area around the fire. "The arsonist might return with another Molotov cocktail!"

Having grown up with a firefighter father, she knew what a Molotov cocktail was, a bottle filled with gas or some other flammable liquid with a wick shoved inside. The cotton wick was started on fire and tossed at something you wanted to burn.

Logically, she knew how it worked, but she'd never seen one up close.

Or been nearly struck by one.

Colin's comment about the arsonist being nearby had her scanning the area intently. There were plenty of people standing around, gaping at the fire as Colin shouted for them to stay back. She didn't see anyone who looked as if they were responsible. Then again, how would she know? The person who'd tossed this bottle wasn't wearing a shirt with the word *arsonist* emblazoned across the chest.

On the heels of that thought came the need to check for injured pedestrians. After scouring the area, she deduced no one had been hurt.

Fire truck sirens wailed as the closest team responded to the blaze. Faye was grateful to note the burn area seemed to be concentrated to where the gasoline had spilled out of the broken bottle. It occurred to her that if they hadn't had that heavy rainstorm two days ago, the fire could have spread much faster, eating up the grass along the way.

Bowing her head for a moment, she gave a quick prayer of thanks that no one else had been injured by a firebomb that was meant for her.

The way this arsonist kept finding her was just as troubling. Glancing at the hotel, she felt certain they couldn't stay there as planned.

Not after this.

Two large firetrucks pulled up in front of the park. Fire-fighters jumped down and began pulling hoses. Two firemen connected their hose to a fire hydrant, while others carried the nozzle toward the fire.

"Let's get out of the way." Colin put his arm around her shoulders and led her in a wide circle away from the blaze.

"I thought water wasn't good to use on gasoline?" She frowned when the firefighters turned the hose on, letting out a stream of water pressurized by the hydrant.

"It's not, but they can drench the grass around the fire to help prevent spread. And they'll use sand and a fire blanket to smother the rest of the flames." Colin's voice was grim. "Are you okay? I didn't hurt you?"

"I'm fine." She wasn't going to complain about bumps and bruises, although she was still sore from the incident in the restroom. "Did you get a look at the person who threw it?"

"No." Colin's scowl deepened. "There were people milling about, though. I saw a couple of skateboarders and bicycle riders. Could have been any of them."

"Maybe someone will come forward with a descrip-tion." She hated to think of the arsonist getting away with this. "It's broad daylight, someone must have seen something."

"I hope you're right." He kept his arm around her shoul-ders as he swept his gaze over the area. "I have a bad feeling this guy is here, watching."

She shivered, despite the warmth. "You need to call Mitch. He shouldn't come near the hotel. It's not safe."

"No, it's not." He did not look at all happy about that. "It doesn't make sense that you were found here, Faye. No one knew we were coming. And if they'd tracked us to the hotel, why not try something there? Why take the risk of tossing a Molotov cocktail at you?"

"I don't know." She was just as frustrated as he was. "I used my credit card on the room, that's the only thing I can come up with as far as how I've been found. But your average arsonist shouldn't be savvy enough to track my credit card payments."

"We're dealing with someone who is smart and a bit desperate. These last two attacks against you come across as impulsive. Maybe even crimes of opportunity." Colin shrugged. "It was easier for him to take a shot at you out here than try to get at you in the hotel."

There was some logic in his theory, so she nodded. "So the next place we go needs to be a place where we can pay cash."

"Yes." He waved a hand. "There's Mitch now."

The tall, blond arson investigator hurried over. "Another attempt to harm Faye?"

"Yep." Colin quickly filled him in. "We need a place where we can stay off-grid."

"The American Lodge?" Mitch offered. "Then again, that's in Brookland and may be too obvious with a retired firefighter running the place."

"Right. We need somewhere else that will allow us to pay cash." Colin reached for his phone. "I think Tarin and Joy stayed in a place a while back."

"No, it's better if there are no ties to your family," Mitch said. "I know of a place, the Sunflower Inn. They'll take cash."

"Okay, thanks. We'll find it."

"Wait, what about the list of patient complaints?" Despite her unwillingness to breach patient privacy, she was eager to do something constructive.

"Right here." Mitch thrust a folded sheet of paper into her hand. "Take a look, see what you think. I'll be in touch once I clear this scene."

"We're not sticking around," Colin warned. "Not when Faye clearly has a target on her back."

"Understood. But since you want to be off-grid, you should probably take my SUV." Mitch tossed Colin the keys. "I'll drive your Jeep. I assume it's in the parking lot of the motel?"

"It is." Colin pulled his keys from his pocket and dropped them in Mitch's palm. "Thanks for the extra help on this. I owe you one."

"Nah, we're family, remember?" Mitch flashed a teasing smile before turning to speak with the firefighting crew.

Faye could tell Colin would rather have stayed to talk to them, too, but he ushered her toward the hotel. "Come on, we need to get out of here."

She quickened her pace to keep up with his long strides. The way he kept her close, his head moving from side to side as he watched for threats, made her feel safe and protected.

As much as she hated to admit it, because she really didn't want him, or anyone for that matter, to be in danger—she needed Colin Finnegan. His support, quick thinking, and sharp reflexes had saved her life several times in the past few hours.

"I really don't understand this." She sighed once they were settled in Mitch's SUV. Colin surprised her by driving up and over a curb to get away from the hotel because the firetrucks had the street blocked off. Apparently, nothing was going to keep him from leaving the area as quickly as possible.

"Look at your list." Colin shot her a glance. "Something

you did or didn't do has to be the motivation here. Once we understand what that is, we can find the person responsible."

"Okay." She unfolded the list of patient names. "Wow, there are twenty-five names here along with a summary of the complaint. I had no idea this many people were upset with me." Her eyes widened. "And this is only the past six months!"

"I expected more," Colin said frankly.

"Why? I'm a good doctor." She was hurt he'd assumed she wasn't doing her best.

"Of course, you are. You know as well as I do that some people blame the doctor when a patient's outcome isn't what they'd hoped for." He smiled reassuringly. "I believe most of those complaints are centered around not wanting to hear what you had to tell them."

"Maybe." She sighed and scanned the names first. Out of the entire list there was only one that she remembered by name, a Martin Steele. He'd come in with stroke symptoms that had been going on for almost eight hours. She'd activated the stroke team and had given care per their stroke protocol, but he had not recovered. As she reviewed the complaint, she read about how the patient's wife, Lavone, blamed her for her husband's left-sided paralysis. The woman went on to say she'd filed a complaint with the medical licensing board too.

She'd felt terrible about Mr. Steele's poor outcome, but she wasn't responsible. The hospital did tons of stroke training throughout the year, especially during May, National Stroke Awareness Month. There were paid commercials as well as flyers that went out to all the households with patients who'd been seen at Trinity Medical Center. The goal was to treat a possible stroke within three hours of the onset of symptoms. Not eight hours. Reading the complaint now, she remembered how upset she'd been to get the initial call about the complaint. Thankfully, the hospital and the medical licensing board had both agreed her care of Mr. Steele was appropriate.

Displaced anger, just as Colin suggested.

Shaking her head, she went back to the top of the list. As much as Mr. Steele's wife was mad at her, she hardly thought the woman was the arsonist. For one thing, the patient was in his sixties, and if she remembered the wife correctly, she was of a similar age. No way had she ridden away on a motor scooter from the park.

A son or daughter? That was a possibility she hadn't considered.

She sighed and continued reading. Some of the complaints were centered around billing, which she under-stood but didn't control. She read every single complaint, finding three patients who were younger men who'd been unhappy with her care. Mostly because they'd had long wait times to see a doctor. Again, not something she could control.

If she were to prioritize the list, she'd put the three younger men low on the totem pole. The more seriously ill patients, like Mr. Steele, or Mrs. Rainey who'd passed away of a heart attack under her care, should be at the top. Maybe their surviving spouses hadn't decided to come after her, but one of their children might have. It seemed a stretch, but the entire situation was illogical.

What if none of the names on the list belonged to the arsonist? They'd be right back to square one.

"Find anything?" Colin asked as he exited the interstate.

"Not really." She waved a hand. "We can talk to Mitch

about a couple of these complaints, but I'd be shocked if anyone from this list is responsible for these fires."

"You didn't take care of any burn patients?"

She frowned, thinking about that. "I did take care of a young man who was injured setting off fireworks around the Fourth of July. He suffered second-degree burns on his right hand, his dominant hand. It was a pretty big deal as far as how his mobility had suffered. People don't realize how much they need their fingers and thumb until they can't use them."

"Do you remember his name?"

She shook her head. "No, and if I did, I couldn't tell you. Patient confidentiality, remember? Besides, I hardly think some guy who'd gotten burned would continue setting fires. Wouldn't he shy away from getting burned again?"

"Not always." Colin shrugged. "I've heard stories of fire-bugs finally getting caught with numerous burn scars as souvenirs of their handiwork."

She stared at him, feeling slightly sick. "That's horrible."

"As my brother Aiden says, it takes all kinds of people to make the world go around." Colin grinned. "Aiden often gets deployed as part of the National Guard. He's done everything from pandemic response to disaster relief to taking on angry mobs."

"Sounds interesting, I guess. I don't remember Aiden very well." She changed the subject, growing tired of talking about theories of how criminal minds worked. In her job, she'd witnessed many patients with serious behavioral health problems. None of them had talked about starting fires, though.

"Aiden and Alanna are twins. They were seventeen when our parents died. You graduated early, so you wouldn't remember them from high school. They started as freshmen my senior year. But you may have seen them around the neighborhood."

"Maybe." Talking about the neighborhood reminded her of her father. He didn't know about the restroom fire or the recent Molotov cocktail. She pulled out her phone, then hesitated. "We should call my dad, but I know he'll want to speak with you. And probably with Mitch Callahan too."

"The motel is up ahead. Let's get settled first, then call."

"Sure." She tried not to sigh when she saw how small the place was. Would they be forced to share a room? It wasn't that she didn't trust Colin, she did. But she hadn't shared living space with anyone since her divorce.

And she wasn't keen to do so again.

One weekend, she reminded herself. She could handle anything for one weekend.

Couldn't she?

"STAY HERE, I'm going to see what I can arrange for us." Colin sent Faye a reassuring smile. "I'll try to get connecting rooms if they have them."

"Whatever they have will be fine."

He shut the door and headed inside. Using Mitch's name helped pave the way with the young desk clerk. After paying for two rooms in cash, he gave the guy an extra fifty dollars for his help.

"Thanks!" The young man brightened. "Let me know if you need anything else."

"Will do." He carried the keys outside, flashing them for Faye to see. Her bright smile made his pulse quicken.

He needed to keep his head screwed on straight. This

was no time to think about how much he liked and admired Faye. How much he'd always liked and admired her.

Better to stay focused on uncovering the identity of the arsonist. He had been a little disappointed in her thoughts about the list of patient complaints. Not that he'd expected it to be easy, but a clue would be nice.

"We're all set." He slid in behind the wheel and handed her one of the keys. "We're in rooms 5 and 6, which are right in the middle of the motel. I was able to pay in cash, so there should be no way for us to be tracked here."

"Thanks, Colin."

Rather than parking in front of the rooms, though, he drove Mitch's SUV around the back. There was a small area beneath a tall, overgrown tree with low branches. He winced as the branches scraped the roof of the car.

"Is this necessary?" Faye asked as he pushed out of the driver's side door.

"Yes. Switching cars was a good start, but from this point forward, we're not taking any chances."

"Okay, I understand." She looked uncertain as she followed him around the building and to the side-by-side rooms.

"Don't forget to unlock your connecting room door," he reminded as he entered his room. She nodded and disappeared into hers.

The place wasn't top-notch the way Faye deserved, but it was clean and smelled fresh. He unlocked his connecting door, waiting for her to do the same.

"Hey. Fancy meeting you here." Her tone was light, but her smile was a bit forced.

"I want you to have your privacy, but I also want to be close by in case this guy does find us and tries to come after you again."

She turned to sit on the edge of the bed. "I know. I'm trying to understand why this guy is using fire to take me out."

"Attention seeking for one thing." He dropped down beside her. "Fires make a big splash in the news. And some people are just drawn to fire."

"Not my patients or their families, though." She pushed the papers at him. "The more I think about it, the more it makes sense that this guy is someone within the fire department. Like that guy Sanders."

"These names are just one avenue for us to explore." He set the list aside. "I happen to agree with you on the fire department. Mitch has been so busy investigating these fires, he hasn't mentioned whether he'd found Jayson Sanders yet."

"Attention seeking," she murmured. "That makes sense. I'm just thankful the Molotov cocktail hadn't hurt or killed any innocent bystanders."

"I'm thankful for that too." She was the target; of that he had no doubt.

"I'll pay you back when this is over," she said in a low voice.

"We're friends, no need to worry about that." He didn't want to take her money. Although maybe part of that was out of duty to her father, who'd helped steer him into firefighting as a career.

She gave him a curious look, no doubt thinking about the fact that despite being neighbors while growing up, they hadn't kept in touch the way friends do. His gaze dropped to her mouth for a moment before he caught himself.

Nope. Not going to think about kissing her. That would be crossing the line, and she needed his protection, not to be worried about him making a move on her.

He abruptly shot to his feet, putting badly needed distance between them. "I should call your father."

She wrinkled her nose but nodded. "Yes, but let me talk to him first." She pulled out her phone. "Dad? It's me, Faye. I'm fine but call me when you get this message, okay?"

He frowned from his position near the connecting doorway. "Odd that he didn't pick up. This is the second time you've had to leave a message."

"He's a busy man." She shrugged. "He'll call. But at least he knows I'm not hurt."

He felt terrible for slamming her to the ground like a rugby player. Better that than being burned by the Molotov cocktail, though.

"What Mitch needs to do is get a list of all the firefighters that have been terminated in the last six months." She tilted her head to the side. "Does he need a subpoena for that too?"

"Yes, he'll need to go through legal channels for that. More so to protect your dad from any hint of impropriety."

"That makes sense. He could be accused of bending the rules because I'm his daughter." She sighed and rubbed the back of her head.

"Are you sure you're okay?" He pushed away from the wall to stand before her. "You hit your head on the ground, didn't you? And how are your hands? You took the gauze off to take a shower."

"My hands are fine, and I have a small bump on my head. Didn't even break the skin."

He lightly pushed her hand out of the way to feel for himself. There was a knot back there, with a bit of swelling. "We need to get some ice on that."

"Ice might help, but my headache isn't that bad."

He headed for the door when her phone rang. Turning back, he could see her father's name on the screen.

"Hey, Dad." She winced and pulled the phone away from her ear. Hearing her father's angry tone, he plucked the phone from her hand.

"Chief Kimble? It's Colin Finnegan."

"I thought you were going to protect her," Dorian roared. "She was involved in two more incidents since we spoke this morning!"

"Yes, sir." He deserved the verbal tongue-lashing but knew he wouldn't be able to have a rational discussion until the chief calmed down. "It's my fault she was caught in the park restrooms. I did see the Molotov cocktail in time to get her out of the way, but I should have expected something like that."

"Finnegan, you're making it difficult for me to stay mad." Dorian's voice sounded worn out and tired now. "I know this isn't really your fault, I'm just trying to understand what's happening."

"Me too, sir."

"No one has Jayson Sanders in custody yet?"

"No, although that may be part of the plan here. Keep starting fires to keep Mitch Callahan tied up with investigating them."

"I've asked Callahan to work with your brother Tarin on this. We need more cops out there looking for Sanders."

"That's a good idea but let me ask you something. Who else might have a grudge against you?"

Dorian Kimble let out a harsh laugh. "Too many to count. Why?"

"It's just one of many theories. We have a list of patient complaints against Faye, but there's nothing that really stands out there. We'll keep digging, but using fire in the first place is more likely a firefighter with a bone to pick with you."

"Then why take it out on my daughter?"

"I don't know, sir, but she's been in the media recently. She's dedicated her life to caring for sick people too."

"Faye is higher profile than me as Fire Chief?" His tone relayed his doubt. "Not sure about that."

"Let me talk to him." Faye held out her hand for the phone, then took a moment to place the call on speaker. "Dad, try to come up with a list of suspects from work. Anyone intent on hurting you would know that striking out at your family would hurt you most of all."

"Yeah, you're right about that," he agreed.

"And you need to make sure Annie is okay. I have Colin here, but Annie needs even more protection. She's just a kid."

"Annie is spending the weekend with a friend, so there's no need to worry about her. You're the one that's been targeted, Faye."

Colin caught Faye's concerned gaze. "But, Dad, who is going to keep Annie safe if this guy does go after her next?"

"Her girlfriend's father is a cop. I have no doubt he'll keep an eye on the girls." Dorian was clearly not worried about his youngest. "Besides, this guy hasn't come near our house or approached Annie in any way. Only you, Faye. Is Finnegan still there?"

"Yes, sir," Colin spoke up.

"I'm counting on you to keep my daughter safe, understand?"

"That's been my mission since this morning, sir."

"Good. Callahan is on the other line. Stay in touch." With that, Faye's father disconnected from the call.

"I don't like knowing Annie is off with a friend." Faye

thrust her fingers through her hair. "If this guy doesn't find me, he might go after her."

Colin crossed over and drew her into his arms, offering a friendly hug. Emphasis on friendly. "I'm sure your dad knows what he's doing. And she has a cop looking after her." He smiled against her hair. "You only have a firefighter protecting you. I'm not even armed."

She laughed into his chest, then tipped her head back to look up at him. A flash of awareness hit hard. He told himself to step back.

But his feet didn't move. No, instead he found himself slowly lowering his head to capture her lush mouth with his.

CHAPTER SEVEN

Colin's kiss was everything she'd always wanted. What she'd dreamed of when they were young and in high school. A wave of longing pushed all rational thought from her brain. Clinging to his broad shoulders, she reveled in his embrace. It was their first kiss, but Colin made her feel cherished in a way Rory never had.

Then he broke off their kiss, breathing heavily. Resting her forehead on his chest, she struggled to get control.

"I'm sorry, Faye." His deep voice rumbled from his chest. "I shouldn't have taken advantage of the situation."

She shook her head, drew in a deep breath, and looked up at him. "You didn't. Do I have to apologize to you for kissing you back?"

"No!" His eyes widened in horror. "Of course not."

A smile tugged at her mouth. "Good. Same goes." She forced herself to take a step back. To pull herself together. "Do you think Mitch will call us when he's finished speaking with my dad?"

"I hope so." Colin's intense brown gaze clung to hers.

She sensed he wanted to say something more, but she wasn't interested in rehashing their potent but brief kiss.

Desperate for something constructive to do, she picked up the discarded list of patient complaints. "I guess it can't hurt to check a few of these out. If only to eliminate them."

"I need Mitch to bring us a computer." He pulled out his phone and thumbed in a text. "We could do some rudimentary searches on these patients who are upset with you, see if any of them remotely fit the general height and weight of the arsonist."

"That works." She reached for the pen sitting on the end table and put check marks next to the top three names. These were the most serious complaints, and while she hadn't done anything wrong, she could see where those involved may believe otherwise. Martin Steele and his wife, Lavone, then a woman by the name of Marsha Rainey who'd come in with shortness of breath who'd abruptly went into cardiac arrest and died, and the third one was a man named Kevin Kuester, who had come in with a broken leg, which had rapidly progressed to compartment syndrome. He'd ended up with long incisions along the sides of his legs to relieve the pressure and had made it clear he wasn't happy with her care.

"Let me see." Colin sat beside her, taking the list. He read the complaints she'd marked and let out a low whistle. "None of these are your fault, Faye. Serious complications, sure, but not the result of medical malpractice."

"Thanks, Colin." She was touched by his words. "The rest of the complaints don't rise to a serious enough level to warrant setting my car, my house, and me on fire."

"You're assuming this guy is a rational human being." Colin shrugged. "That's not necessarily the case."

"Okay, but throwing a Molotov cocktail because he

waited too long to be seen? Or because he felt the care wasn't what he'd wanted?" No matter how irrational someone might be, she couldn't see it. "Keep in mind, these are the type of patient complaints everyone gets, not just me."

"Yeah, you have a point there. It makes sense to start with the top three," he admitted. His phone vibrated, and he looked at it for a moment, then turned to show her the screen. "Mitch is finishing up at the crime scene."

"Is he coming here?" She glanced at the parking lot outside the window. "If the arsonist does know your Jeep, that wouldn't be smart."

"He's going to call first." On cue, his phone vibrated again. He put the call on speaker for her benefit. "Hey, Mitch. Find anything helpful?"

"Not really." Mitch sounded tired. "I interviewed several witnesses who all agree they saw a person dressed in black riding a bike toss the bottle toward you and Faye. But that's where the description similarities ended. One woman claimed the rider was an Asian man; another man thought the rider was a woman. A third witness is absolutely positive the rider was a young white male." He sighed. "Take your pick."

"Young white male fits the arsonist profile," Colin said.

"Yes, ninety percent of all arsonists are young white men. But the bottom line is, we don't have anything solid to go on."

"I really think you need to get a list of firefighters who were terminated from the job in the past few months." She met Colin's gaze. "I take it you haven't found Jayson Sanders?"

"Not yet. You should know that we have MPD involved

in searching for him too," Mitch said. "Tarin issued a BOLO for him."

"I went through the patient complaint list, and there are three possibilities to explore." She paused, then added, "I know you're sick of hearing this, but I still think this is related in some way to my dad."

"I just spoke with your father, Faye," Mitch said. "We are exploring that avenue too."

Hearing that was a relief. "Good."

"Do you need anything?" Mitch asked.

"A computer would be nice, but I don't think you should drive here in the Jeep," Colin said. "I'll call one of my siblings."

"I already swapped rides with my brother Marc," Mitch admitted. "I asked him to switch since I knew I'd need to come talk to you. I'll bring a laptop, no problem."

"You rock, cuz." Colin grinned. "Tell Marc we appreciate his support too."

"Hey, we Callahans are happy to help," Mitch assured them. "Give me about an hour or so, okay?"

"Sounds good." She gave Colin a wry smile. "We're not going anywhere."

Mitch chuckled. "See you soon."

"Later," Colin said, before punching the button to end the call. They were still sitting next to each other in the small confines of the motel room.

An hour suddenly seemed like a really long time.

"I'm going to walk around outside for a bit." As if the sense of togetherness was getting to Colin, too, he jumped to his feet. "I won't be long."

"Sure." She watched as he walked through the connecting doorway. Letting out a sigh, she dropped backward onto the bed, staring up at the ceiling.

Obviously, Colin was sticking close to appease her father. He'd said as much when her dad had told him to keep her safe.

This weird awareness between them didn't mean anything. If they hadn't been forced to spend time together, that kiss wouldn't have happened.

She closed her eyes, reining in her emotions. Her schedule was brutal, especially in the summer. Even if she wanted to see Colin after this nightmare was over, she didn't see that happening anytime soon. Especially since his schedule wasn't much better.

And that was assuming he'd be interested. Guys like Colin could have any woman they wanted. Young, hot firefighters did not need to search hard for dates.

She abruptly sat up as a terrible thought hit. What if Colin was seeing someone? No, he would have told her. Wouldn't he?

Yes, he would have. Colin wasn't like Rory. He'd never kiss her if he was seriously involved with someone else.

She put a hand over her heart, willing her pulse to return to normal. Enough. This was hardly the time to think about having a relationship. Not when a vicious arsonist had her in his sights.

Rising to her feet, she peered through the window. The same two cars she'd noticed earlier were still there. No one was lurking nearby. Colin walked around the perimeter of the parking lot, then disappeared behind the building.

They were safe. At least for now.

But she couldn't help feeling as if this peaceful interlude was nothing more than the calm before the storm.

NEEDING SPACE, and a cool head, Colin walked around the property. He wasn't worried that the arsonist was lurking nearby, but sitting next to Faye with her wildflower scent wafting toward him made him want to kiss her again.

Even imagining her fire chief father standing over them wasn't enough to shake the temptation. Man, he had it bad. Wrong place, wrong time, wrong—*everything*.

Faye was in danger from some jerk who not only thought it was fun to start fires, but whose desire for revenge or retribution was escalating rapidly. Colin needed to keep his head screwed on straight.

No more kissing Faye.

He found himself repeating that mantra as he searched the grove of trees behind the building. Maybe if he said the words often enough, he'd find the strength and willpower to heed them.

He didn't find anything suspicious in the woods or around the motel. He walked to the front and used his key to head inside. Faye was in her room, hopefully getting some rest, so he decided to take a shower. A cold one.

When he emerged fifteen minutes later, he saw a missed call from his brother Rhy. Grabbing the phone, he called him back. "Hey, what's up?"

"What's this about a Molotov cocktail?" Rhy demanded. "And why am I hearing that from Miles Callahan rather than you?"

Figures the Callahan grapevine worked just as quickly as their Finnegan one. Miles was an MPD detective as well as being Mitch's brother. Miles must have heard the news from Tarin. "I didn't want to bother you. We're fine. Mitch is doing his part."

"I don't like it," Rhy muttered. "This guy is out of control."

Since he agreed, there was no point in arguing. "We're staying off-grid, Rhy. In a no-name motel room paid for with cash. No need for you to worry."

"Yeah, well, I can't help it. You're not a cop. If this guy escalates from fires to bullets . . ."

"I'll handle it." He didn't appreciate his brother's dig about his not being a cop. "And he hasn't resorted to bullets yet."

"How are you going to stop him if you find him?" Rhy demanded. "Especially if he happens to be carrying?"

To be fair, he hadn't thought that far ahead. Not that he'd give Rhy the satisfaction of hearing that. "Mitch will be here soon with a computer so we can dig into some possible suspects. And Mitch is armed."

"I should have given you a weapon when you were here at the homestead," Rhy grumbled. "You know we have a couple of handguns and ammo in the safe."

Yeah, he knew that, but he hadn't thought of grabbing one. He knew how to shoot; his older siblings had made sure of that. He'd been to the firing range often enough over the years. As much as he hated to admit it, Kyleigh had been a better shot than he was by a mile. Watching her nailing the center of her target only made him realize his choice to become a firefighter and paramedic had been the right one. He hated to admit he wouldn't have made it as a cop. "Have faith, Rhy. We'll be fine."

"You'd better be fine." It was a comical threat. "I don't want to hear about you or Faye being hurt, understand?"

"I'll do my best." His older siblings had all been in danger over the past few months, and it made him wonder if Rhy had threatened them the same way. Even Rhy himself had put his life on the line to protect Devon. It was a little strange that Colin was in the center of danger now, despite his job not being involved in law enforcement.

"Keep me updated, Colin. No more hearing about dangerous situations through the family grapevine."

"That's the plan." He shook his head at how his brother still played the role of their father, even ten years later. Since he'd appreciated what Rhy and Tarin had given up to hold things together, he let it go. "Later."

"Any news?" Faye asked from the doorway.

"Not yet." He gestured for her to come inside. "I was hoping you were getting some sleep."

"Better to stay up in case we actually get to sleep tonight." She offered a half smile. "I'm on days next week, so it would be nice to get back on a normal sleeping schedule."

"I know how you feel. If we have a rough night, I try to stay awake as long as possible the next day." He ran his fingers through his damp hair, hoping and praying the arsonist was caught by Monday morning. "Switching from nights to days back to nights again is tough."

"Part of the job." She sank down on the edge of the bed. "I'm not used to being idle. Normally I'd be working on all the chores I'd neglected while working five shifts straight. This sitting around is driving me batty."

"I hear you." He sat in the chair. "This isn't usual for me either."

"You live alone?" she asked.

"Yes, I do now. When I first moved out of the homestead, I shared a place with one of my colleagues." He grimaced. "That was fine when we were in our early twenties. John liked to party, but that grew old after a while. John kept bugging me to go out, to be his wingman. I wasn't that interested in the bar scene, so I saved up until I could buy a place of my own."

"You're not lonely? I mean, you grew up with eight siblings. It must be strange living alone."

"I'm not lonely at all. I spend enough time at the fire-house with the rest of the team." It dawned on him what she was really asking. "I had a girlfriend for a while, which was nice, but Luanne decided to move south. I didn't want to leave my family, so we parted ways amicably." He held her gaze. "What about you?"

"You know about my failed marriage. I don't mind living alone. Now my house is gone . . ." Her voice trailed off.

"Hey, I'm sure your insurance company will come through for you. On both your house and your car."

"I hope so." She turned to glance out the window. He heard the car engine, too, and was silently relieved to know Mitch had arrived. He went over to peek through the curtains to verify his assumption, then opened the door for the arson investigator.

"Hey." Mitch pulled a laptop carrying case from the front seat, then opened the back to remove a pack of bottled water. "I was able to get here sooner than I thought."

"Perfect." The less togetherness with Faye, the better. "Did you find anything new?"

"I got the list of terminated firefighters." Mitch grinned. "I think Faye is onto something with this being an attempt to lash out at her father through her. The three of us need to review the names together."

"Better than doing nothing. Come on." He stepped back to give Mitch room to enter, then grabbed the water from him. "Make yourself at home."

"I can't wait to look at the list of terminated firefighters."

Faye's eyes lit up with anticipation as she accepted a bottle of water from him. "I'm sure our guy is on that list."

The three of them crowded around the small table. Mitch tapped his finger on the first name. "Jayson Sanders is the top suspect, of course. But there are six others who were let go over the past six months."

"Only six, or rather seven?" Colin found that low number surprising. "For the entire city?"

"And the suburbs, too, since so many of us work for more than one station." Mitch had once been a firefighter paramedic just like Colin. "Honestly, I expected more names as well. Then again, I'd like to believe firefighters are in general honorable men and women. If we go back further, say a year, there would likely be more. But the judge didn't like that idea and only gave us permission to get the names of those who were let go in the past six months, that was all he approved for Faye's patient complaints, too. If we can get evidence that indicates for sure this is the work of a former firefighter, he agreed to expand the subpoena."

"Any women on the list?" Faye asked.

"No." Mitch tilted his head. "Why, are you thinking the perp is a female?"

"Not necessarily." She grimaced. "The camera footage in the parking structure wasn't much help. It could have been a larger woman or a smaller man."

"All six are men," Mitch said. "And other than Jayson Sanders, the remaining five men are in their midtwenties, which is interesting as far as a firefighter turning arsonist. Jayson at thirty-four is a bit older than the usual firebug."

"But he has the biggest motivation," Colin argued. "A personal grudge against Chief Dorian Kimble."

"Yep. But we should look at these other guys too." Mitch pulled the computer out and opened it.

"Is there a reason attached to the termination?" Faye asked. "That may help."

"No, unfortunately. Most are simply listed for cause," Mitch explained. "We only know the reason for Jayson's termination because your father filled us in."

"Seems like we're working blindfolded," she muttered.

"This from a woman who didn't want to breach patient privacy," Colin teased.

"We already have the cops looking for Jayson," Mitch said, getting back to the subject at hand. "If we search their social media sites, we may find a reason to move one of these other guys higher on the suspect list."

"The glory of arson investigation," Colin said with a sigh.

"Tell me about it." Mitch shook his head. "The scene outside the courthouse didn't give me anything useful. The restroom fire was interesting since the accelerant was paint thinner, not gasoline, which was the substance used in the Molotov cocktail."

"What about my car fire? Which accelerant was used there?" Faye asked.

"Paint thinner as well. Could be that this guy is trying to switch things up to keep us off balance. Typical arsonists use the same signature for each fire, this perp isn't doing that. Unfortunately, I don't know enough about your house fire yet because the scene was still hot when I went by on my way here." His expression darkened. "I know this much: an accelerant was used, and the fire was likely started in the basement. I think the perp must have chosen to place the blaze close to the gas line, hoping for an explosion."

The explosion that had caused Larry's death. If that was the goal, it certainly worked. In fact, it was nothing short of a miracle that the blast hadn't killed more of them. Colin clenched his jaw, then tried to let go of the anger. They'd find this guy, and when they did? He'd spend the rest of his life in prison for murder.

Faye frowned. "I always lock my doors, so this guy must have broken a window to get inside."

"Were your basement windows locked?" Colin asked. "We sometimes find those smaller windows are overlooked."

"Yes, they're always locked too. As an ED doctor and a woman living alone, I'm careful that way. Especially after my divorce."

Colin sent her a sharp look. "You were afraid of your ex?"

"Not physically afraid, but I knew he was upset at the judge's decision and didn't want to come home to find him waiting for me." She flushed, then added, "Since the arsonits broke my car window, it's not a stretch to believe he broke one of the windows in my house. I'm surprised none of the neighbors noticed anything strange, though."

Mitch shrugged. "Last I checked in, the local police were still canvassing the area. It's possible someone could still come forward with information. Looking at the timeline, the perp was gone from the parking garage by the time you went to your vehicle. He was probably already on his way to your place while Colin's crew was extinguishing that blaze. The hour was still early enough that many people wouldn't have noticed his approaching your house, especially if he went in around back."

"I'm sure the canvass will come up with something." Colin lightly touched Faye's hand. "We'll get to the bottom of this."

"I know." She shifted her gaze from him toward the window. "I hope it's soon."

"Faye, you need to review these names first." Mitch

pushed the list toward her. "I'd like to know if any of these people sound familiar."

She nodded and did what he asked. After a minute, she shook her head. "Sorry, they mean nothing to me."

"No connection to your ex-husband?" Mitch asked.

"Not that I'm aware of." She pursed her lips. "Rory didn't have a lot of friends. Other than his former college roommates."

"Will you write those names down for us?" Mitch stood and grabbed the pad of paper near the phone.

While Faye was writing down her ex-husband's college roommates, Colin reached for the list of terminated firefighters. "Did any of these names ring a bell with you, Mitch?"

"No." He shrugged. "I haven't been on duty in a fire station for a while, though."

Colin scanned the names, his gaze homing in on the last one. "Daniel Percy."

"You know him?" Mitch leaned forward. "Did he work out of your house?"

Colin nodded. "He was only with us for a little over a year, though, before he transferred out." He tried to remember more about the brash and cocky kid. "He was smart enough, knew his medical training inside and out. But when it came to firefighting, he didn't take well to being told what to do. Not exactly what I'd call a team player."

"That's good insight." Mitch opened a browser on the computer and began looking for Daniel Percy's social media sites. "Sounds like he may have a grudge against authority if he ultimately lost his job over his attitude."

"You know, I think Daniel mentioned having a brother on the job." He drummed his fingers, trying to remember their brief interactions. "Something about how fighting fires runs in his blood."

"Maybe his dad was also on the job." Mitch looked excited to have a possible suspect.

"His dad may not have gotten along with my dad," Faye added. She straightened and grabbed Colin's arm. "My dad was given his promotion three years ago. It could be that one of the guys who was passed over is still angry over that."

"That's a really good point, Faye." Mitch flashed a smile. "Here, I think I may have found one of Daniel's sites." He turned the computer so Colin could see the profile picture. "Is that the same guy you worked with?"

"Yep. That's him." He frowned. "I wish I could remember his brother's name. I'm sure he mentioned it at some point."

"Maybe we can find his brother here." Mitch grinned. "It's always nice when these guys don't bother to make their sites private. I can see all his friends, here."

Colin grimaced. "He has a lot. Start with his posts. From what I remember about Daniel, he's the type to vent about losing his job, complaining that the upper brass had it out for him, rather than taking accountability for his actions."

"Hang on a minute," Mitch protested. Their gazes locked for a moment. "Are you seeing what I'm seeing?"

Colin nodded slowly. "Jayson Sanders is one of his friends." Then it clicked. "Wait a minute, Daniel's older brother."

"They have different last names," Faye pointed out.

"That's because they have different fathers." He stared at Mitch. "Daniel told me his mother had remarried after a divorce. Jayson and Daniel could be working together. Two half brothers determined to make Chief Kimble pay for the way they both lost their jobs."

"This connection is impossible to ignore. And it would explain the different accelerants used in the fires." Mitch tapped the screen. "As far as I'm concerned, Daniel and Jayson are both at the top of our suspect list."

It was a good lead. These two men needed to be found before they had a chance to strike again.

CHAPTER EIGHT

Faye felt sick to her stomach. It was horrifying to think about the way these two former firefighter brothers had targeted her to lash back at her father. She sent up a quick prayer that God would keep Annie safe from harm. Better for her to be in danger than her younger half sister.

She watched as Mitch brought their photographs up on the screen. Both men were muscular, from what she could see while they wore their firefighter uniforms, but Daniel, the younger of the two, seemed heavier than the person she'd seen on the hospital video.

"I'm calling this in," Mitch said. "I'd like proof that Jayson and Daniel are in fact half brothers. From there, maybe we can get a search warrant for their phones."

"Sounds like a good plan," Colin agreed. He flashed her a reassuring smile. "Your life will get back to normal once we have these two in custody."

She nodded, even though her new normal meant having no house and no car. Obviously, her life was more important than those two things. Colin's life was too. And she still had her career as a physician, so there was no reason to feel sorry for herself. That said, she truly hoped Mitch could get these guys' phone records. If they had coordinated a planned attack, surely they'd have texted or called each other to pull this off.

Mitch stood and walked outside to make his call, leaving her and Colin alone. She gestured toward the computer screen. "What do you think? Should we update my dad on this latest information?"

Colin considered that for a moment. "Not yet. Let's wait until we have something more concrete. It's okay for us to jump to conclusions and investigate these two as our top suspects, but they are both innocent until proven guilty."

"Yes, you're right." She understood his reluctance. It would be better for Colin to call her dad with a specific lead rather than supposition.

"Are you hungry?" Colin asked. "When we're finished here, we can grab something to eat."

"I'd like that." She had enjoyed their lunch until the Molotov cocktail had nearly hit them. "As long as you think we're safe."

"I'm fairly confident we weren't followed." He jerked his thumb to the door where Mitch was still in deep conversation with whoever would be getting the subpoena for their suspects' phone records. "He's armed."

Faye wasn't a big fan of guns. Working in the ED meant having patients rolling through with various gunshot wounds on a regular basis. Sometimes they had several patients in one shift. Yet she had an appreciation for those who protected the public. Her father and Colin had taken the path of fighting fires, but she'd cared for enough police officers to have the utmost respect for them too.

"I'm not worried." She did her best to smile. "I have

confidence Mitch will find those responsible. And he may want to join us for dinner too."

"He's more than welcome, but I suspect he'll want to head back to Milwaukee to serve the warrant." Colin glanced over as Mitch returned.

The grin on the investigator's face was a good sign. "We got the approval for the warrant. I hate to leave you guys here, but I need to get back." He looked at her. "Are you sure those who lodged patient complaints shouldn't be investigated more thoroughly?"

"We can look at their social media sites." She shrugged. "It will give us something to do, but I do not believe they're involved. It's too big of a stretch that one of them would use fire to strike out at me."

"I tend to agree," Mitch said. "But maybe dig a little deeper just in case. Maybe one of them has a connection to a firefighter. Stranger things have happened."

"We'll do that." Colin stood. "After dinner. Would you like to join us?"

"I wish I could. I'll grab something along the way." Mitch arched a brow. "No time to linger, Chief wants results."

Faye wanted to point out that her father wasn't such a hard taskmaster that he'd expect Mitch to skip dinner but sensed that was just an excuse. Mitch clearly wanted to hit the road with this new information and to impress her father. She couldn't blame him. Obviously, her father's opinion carried a lot of weight throughout the department.

"Will you keep us updated?" Colin asked.

"Of course. You'll be the first to know if we make an arrest." Mitch hesitated, then bent over to tie his shoe.

No, that wasn't what he was doing. He straightened

holding a gun and ankle holster in hand. "I know you don't have a carry permit, but I think you should be armed."

"I do have a permit," Colin corrected. "But I don't carry a gun."

"Take it." Mitch pressed the weapon into his hand. "For my peace of mind, and Chief Kimble's too. You and Faye are in danger. At the very least, you can use the gun to scare them off."

With a sigh, Colin accepted the weapon. "Okay, for Faye's sake, I'll take it."

His comment made her feel guilty. She didn't want him to carry the gun unless he was comfortable with it.

"Good." Mitch grinned again. "You know, if you ever decide to go the investigator route, I'll put in a good word for you."

Colin chuckled at that. "I have no plans to give up my position, Callahan. But thanks for the suggestion and support."

"Suit yourself." Mitch shot her a curious glance, making her wonder if her complicated feelings for Colin were obvious, before turning to head out the motel room door.

Resisting the urge to cover her warm cheeks flush with embarrassment, she turned back to the computer. Mitch wanted her top three patient complaints checked out, so that's what she'd do.

"We can do that after dinner," Colin pointed out.

"Just give me a few minutes." She didn't look up at him, lest he notice her feelings too. "This won't take long."

"Okay." He crowded close. Too close. After seeing how Mitch and Colin had used Jayson's social media site, she did the same with the first name on her list, Martin and Lavone Steele. Lavone had a page; Martin didn't. She was able to find several family photos, and it was clear their children were too large to be the suspect on the videotape.

"One down, two to go." She typed in the next name. That suspect was also just as quickly ruled out, at least in her humble opinion. After searching the third name, she found one son who fit the description. But when she dug deeper, she discovered the guy was currently living in Kentucky.

"He could be here visiting," she said to Colin. "But I doubt it. Looks like he has a full-time job in accounting. Not exactly the type to start fires."

"We'll jot his name down as a possible." Colin took the pad of paper and made a note. "I agree with you, though. I don't see this guy as our suspect."

Sitting back in the chair, she stared at the screen. It was looking more and more likely that Jayson and Daniel were responsible. With a grimace, she closed the laptop. "We should grab dinner."

"Yes, let's." Colin stood. "I searched for nearby restaurants while you were poking through social media sites. There's a Mexican place three miles from here."

"Yum." She liked all different types of food. Especially if she didn't have to cook it. "I'm ready."

He surprised her by taking her hand. He'd grabbed the laptop, too, maybe planning to do more searches. They walked around the corner of the building to reach the back where he'd left Mitch's SUV. Mitch had borrowed his brother's vehicle, who was now driving Colin's Jeep. It was like musical SUVs around here.

Colin drove while keeping one eye glued to the rearview mirror. She appreciated his intense scrutiny but felt safe here with him. They'd taken every precaution possible. If they weren't safe here, she wasn't sure they'd be safe anywhere.

She tried not to dwell on the grim thought.

The three-mile drive took longer than normal because Colin backtracked several times. His actions, and the weapon strapped to his ankle, made him come across as a keen-eyed cop.

When he'd parked near the exit of the restaurant, she put a hand on his arm. "You're not going to wear the gun inside, are you?"

"Oh, yeah. I am." He didn't smile.

"I can tell you're not comfortable with it," she protested. "No need to take it inside."

"How I feel doesn't matter. Anything that keeps you from being hurt is worth it. Besides, it's well hidden under my jeans at my ankle." He pushed open his door. "Let's go."

She sighed and slid out of the vehicle. Colin held the door open for her, taking one last look over his shoulder before following her inside.

They were seated at a small booth in the corner. Colin took the seat facing the door.

"You really have a concealed carry permit?" She eyed him over the rim of their plastic menu.

"I do. And I'm okay at hitting my target." The corner of his mouth lifted in a rueful smile. "Not as good as my sister Kyleigh, though. She's crazy accurate. As are my brothers, Rhy, Tarin, Brady, Quinn, and Aiden. They used to tease me that I inherited my lack of skill in target practice from our mother."

She smiled. "I'm sure you're skilled enough. But seriously, please don't use the gun unless you really have to." She paused, then added, "I admire your career choice of being a firefighter. It doesn't matter to me if you can shoot like your brothers and sister."

"Trust me, I won't use it unless absolutely necessary." Colin looked up as their server approached. They gave their orders, sticking with soft drinks rather than one of their blended margaritas.

She toyed with her water glass. "It's hard to believe we've only reconnected this morning. It's been a really long day."

"Hey, I'm here for you." He reached across the table to take her hand. "We're going to get through this, Faye. You'll be safe, I promise. I don't think it will be long now before Mitch gets Jayson and Daniel in custody."

"I know." She stared at their clasped hands, realizing the hours she'd spent with Colin only reinforced how bad her marriage to Rory had been, even before she'd caught him cheating. Colin was an honorable man.

The careful way his strong fingers curled around hers made her wish for things she couldn't have.

———

COLIN KNEW he was in way over his head. His former admiration for Faye was messing with his mind. He released her hand, then sat back in the booth. A thought occurred to him. "Did your stepmother ever call you back?"

"Claire? No." She shrugged. "I'm sure she knows my dad and I have been in touch. No reason for her to call too."

"Faye, you were almost burned to death and hit by a Molotov cocktail." He scowled. "That's plenty reason for her to call you."

"Claire and I get along fine, but she's never been motherly toward me. Even though I was twelve when they married, she had Annie two years later and was focused on her. Getting into college early was helpful. Once I was out of the house, we didn't see each other often. If anything, she's been more of a distant older sister."

"Distant and sister are not congruent," he pointed out.

"Not all families are like the Finnegans," she shot back. "Trust me, I see dysfunctional families in the ED all the time."

He nodded. She was right, he knew most families weren't as tightly knit as the Finnegans and Callahans. Still, he'd have thought Claire would have checked in with her stepdaughter in a time of crisis. "I'm sure you do. But illness often brings out the worst in people."

"As do other emergencies." Faye glanced up as their server arrived. "Wow, everything looks good."

His mouth watered at the sizzling steak fajitas. Faye had ordered fish tacos, and her meal looked good too. When their server left, he once again reached for her hand. "I'll say grace."

"I'd like that." She smiled and bowed her head. He was glad she didn't mind participating in Finnegan traditions.

"Dear Lord Jesus, thank You for this wonderful food we are blessed to eat. Please continue to keep Faye safe in Your loving care and give us the strength and wisdom to seek justice. Amen."

"Amen," she repeated, then she met his gaze. "I get the sense you pray even when you're not in danger."

"All the time," he admitted.

She nodded thoughtfully, then dug into her tacos. He did the same, enjoying the steak fajitas. They were halfway through their meal when Callahan texted him.

"What is it?" She craned her neck to see across the table.

"Mitch has the warrant, but there's no sign of Jayson or Daniel at their respective homes." He should have known it wouldn't be so easy. "Don't worry, they can't hide for long."

"Surprisingly, I'm not worried." She smiled. "Hard to be concerned when I have you and God watching over me."

"Truth." He thumbed a quick response, then slipped the phone back into his pocket.

Faye frowned and looked around the bench seat. "Rats. I forgot to bring my purse and phone."

"I'll take care of the bill." Maybe he was being too macho, but he'd rather pay for their meals. It wasn't like they were on a date, but he still didn't like taking her money. He figured she'd need everything she had to pay her house and car deductibles for the insurance company.

"I'll pay for our next meal." She huffed a bit, then continued eating. He decided not to argue, even though he had no intention of letting that happen.

After a few more minutes of eating, she frowned. "Where do you think Jayson and Daniel are hiding out?"

"Could be anywhere, but I suspect they're driving around looking for clues as to where you might be."

"But the person at the park was on a motor scooter. And the Molotov cocktail was tossed by someone riding a bike."

"Yes, and the person at the hospital parking garage was seen sprinting away, either to a car or some other form of transportation outside camera view," he agreed. "Looking back, it's easy to see how these two may have split up to make several attempts against you. Thankfully, they failed, which is a blessing." He firmly believed God was watching over them.

"Yes, it is," she whispered.

"By now, though, I'm sure the half brothers are sticking together." It wasn't at all reassuring to think of the damage two arsonists could do by working as a team. He tried not to show his deep concern over what might happen if they did find Faye. "Don't worry, I doubt they'll be able to hide for long. Since Mitch attained a subpoena and warrant to look at their phones, I'm sure the cops have issued a BOLO on their vehicles."

"Be on the lookout," she murmured, using her fork to spear a stray piece of avocado. "I guess that means every squad is looking for them, right?"

"Right." He knew it wasn't quite that easy. Unfortunately, there was a significant amount of crime in the city, and those calls would always take priority over a BOLO. If the brothers were smart, that's where they'd hang out. But he hoped they'd choose to stay closer to one of their residences where they'd be more likely to be found.

"Well, that's reassuring, I guess." She didn't seem convinced. And he didn't blame her. Not after the past few hours of nonstop danger.

"They'll also get the phone records from the carrier if needed." He glanced at his watch, wincing when he saw it was well past business hours on a Friday night. "But that may take time."

"I know." Faye finished the last of her tacos, pushing her plate away. "Thanks, Colin. That was good."

"Mine too." He pulled out some cash to pay their tab. He wouldn't have minded lingering at the restaurant, but when Faye yawned, he decided it was better that they both try to get some sleep.

As much as he hated to admit it, he didn't think Mitch would make much progress on the case yet tonight. Especially if the BOLO didn't pick up the half-brothers' vehicle. Without the phones themselves, Mitch would have to wait until morning to get the upper brass to convince the phone company to provide records on a Saturday.

No easy task. But he had no doubt that with Chief Kimble's daughter at the center of danger, Mitch would get what he needed.

Once the bill was paid, he led the way outside. Just like on the ride here, he took a moment to survey the area, searching for anything suspicious.

With the sun dipping low on the horizon, the air wasn't nearly as hot and thick with humidity as it had been earlier. Fighting fires in the summer was never fun; the heat became that much more intense when you had scorching temps to deal with.

Once they were settled in Mitch's SUV, he headed back out on the highway, in the opposite direction from where their motel was located. Faye didn't complain about the extra drive. She stared out the window, seemingly lost in her thoughts.

He wanted to ask more about her failed marriage but forced himself to hold his tongue. Her personal life wasn't any of his business. Not to mention, he had his own failed relationships too. Luanne had accused him of putting his family first, and truthfully, she'd been right. Looking back, he could see where he'd gone wrong. And maybe he hadn't cared about Luanne enough to make her a priority.

Yet Faye's ex-husband's cheating wasn't her fault. And if the idiot wasn't involved, then it was best to let it be.

"I don't think Claire likes to see me because I'm a reminder that my father had loved someone else." She turned from the window to look at him. "I guess I didn't push for a closer relationship either, although I did try to keep in touch with Annie."

"The age gap between you and Annie must have made that difficult."

"Yes. It was great when she was a baby, and I helped take care of her a lot. But over time my undergraduate studies, medical school, and residency schedules made our gatherings less frequent. I barely make half the holidays."

"But you see your dad more often, don't you?" He couldn't imagine not being close with his family.

"Yes." She broke into a wide smile. "He's dropped by to have dinner with me at the Trinity Medical Center cafeteria. How's that for dedication? The hospital is nice, but they don't serve gourmet food by any stretch of the imagination. After working there through my three-year residency and now three years as a physician, I can barely eat there. I bring my lunch most of the time."

"No one goes hungry at the firehouse," he joked. "Sometimes the food is cold by the time we return from a call out, but there's always food available."

When he was certain they weren't followed or drawing any curious attention, he turned and doubled back toward the motel. He planned to park in the trees behind the building again, just to be on the safe side. Hopefully, by this time tomorrow, the half brothers would no longer be a threat.

The more he thought about his time with Faye ending, though, the more tempting it was to ask her out once this was over. Would she be interested in a guy like him? She probably made more than triple his salary.

Money didn't buy happiness, and truthfully, the Finnegan family was living proof. It had taken hard work from both Rhy and Tarin to hold the family together. The life insurance was enough to cover most of the mortgage on the house, but that didn't account for daily living expenses for a large family or annual property taxes.

No, money couldn't bring their parents back. And he'd learned from his older siblings who'd all found their better halves over the past year that love and family trumped everything.

He drove past the motel once, noting that some of the cars parked out front had changed. New guests arriving for the weekend most likely. After circling around, he drove around to the back of the building.

Darkness had fallen now that the hour was past eight o'clock. It wasn't as easy to see without streetlights or illumination from the motel windows. That didn't prevent him from parking in the same spot he'd used earlier.

After sliding out from behind the wheel, he ducked beneath the low-hanging branches and went around to take Faye's hand.

"The ground is rocky back here," he warned.

"I figured." She let him help her cross the uneven terrain. Then she stopped to stare up at the starlit sky. "It's pretty."

He fought the urge to kiss her again. "Yeah, it is."

They headed around to the front of the motel. He noticed there was a car parked in front of Faye's room, but since there was loud laughter coming from the room beside hers, he wasn't alarmed.

"We may have to swap rooms." He nodded at the partially open doorway of room seven. "Sounds like they're not going to sleep anytime soon, and you need your rest."

"So do you." She sighed. "Hopefully, they'll call it quits at a decent hour."

He hated to be the type of customer who complained about the noise, but if those motel room residents didn't shut it down by ten, he would complain. He stopped in front of his door and dug out his key.

"I can't believe I left my purse and phone here," Faye said. "And my key."

"At least we have connecting rooms." He unlocked the door, then stepped back so she could go in first.

A loud whooshing noise had him instinctively grabbing her arm. "Faye!"

She stumbled back against him, lifting her free arm to block her face from the fire. "My room is burning!"

Colin had no idea how this had happened, but he didn't waste time figuring it out. He tugged her outside and fished in his pocket for the car keys. "Get the SUV, hurry!"

"What about you?" Faye asked, coughing from the smoke she'd inhaled.

"I have to get those other people out of there." He didn't want to leave her alone, but the partygoers in room seven were in real danger. "Hurry."

She did as he asked, rushing around the corner of the building to get the SUV. He rushed toward room seven and threw the door open without bothering to knock. "Fire! You need to get outside, now!"

"Fire?" One guy stared at him in confusion. There were several empty beer bottles scattered around, which likely contributed to his clouded judgment. "Where?"

"In room six, next door. Move it, now! You all need to get outside!" If they didn't start walking under their own power, he'd be forced to carry them out.

Thankfully, one of the party attendees, a woman dressed in tiny shorts and a tank top, came out of the bathroom. "Hey, it's smoky in there."

"Fire!" One of the other women bolted toward the door.

It was as if a sieve opened up as the other occupants of the room quickly followed.

Satisfied to have them outside, he went up and down the row of rooms, banging on doors and yelling fire to anyone who might be inside. Faye pulled up in the SUV, her face pale as people huddled together far from the fire that could now be seen lapping at the walls and curtains.

When he was reassured all the innocent people were out of harm's way, he jumped into the passenger seat. "Go, hurry."

Faye hit the gas, sending the SUV lurching forward. Seconds later, they were back out on the highway.

He lightly punched his armrest, mentally kicking himself for not expecting this. Although they'd gone to such pains not to be followed. How in the world . . .

Then it hit him. Faye's cell phone. She'd left it behind in the room.

The same room engulfed by flames.

CHAPTER NINE

Gripping the steering wheel tightly, Faye hit the gas, driving away from the burning motel. If she hadn't forgotten her purse and key, she'd have walked right into the burning room. The thought of being hit in the face by the fire made her stomach churn. As a doctor, she knew all too well how burn victims suffered.

"How?" The word came out in a croak. She hadn't inhaled much smoke, not like during the time she'd been locked in the Brookland Park restroom, but her face felt hot, possibly slightly burned from the fire that had come through the opened connecting door with the abrupt influx of oxygen.

"Your phone, although your average firefighter doesn't have the ability to track cell phone numbers." Colin shook his head. "Even if these guys are working together, it doesn't make sense that they'd have found you here."

"I figured my phone must have been how they found my location, but how did they get into the room to start the fire?" She darted a quick glance at Colin, before focusing back on the road. "The desk clerk wouldn't give out our key.

And if they knew I wasn't in the room, why bother setting it on fire?"

"Those are good questions," Colin admitted. "I need to call Mitch, see if he has any ideas. I haven't heard of anyone starting a fire using the crack beneath the door, although I noticed these doors are worn to the point where there was plenty of outside light seeping underneath. With a special kind of accelerant and delivery system, not to mention sheer determination, it may be possible."

She swallowed hard. "You think they believed me to be inside?"

"I do, yes. Most people are attached to their phones, right? And there was a vehicle from the party room parked in front of your door." Colin grimaced and added, "The noisy neighbors may have helped cover any noise the arsonist made while starting the fire."

"That's horrifying." After being stuck in the bathroom, she'd known that the escalating attacks meant they wanted to physically harm her, but the reality of what might have happened if she had been inside brought a wave of nausea. She didn't like fire. She was afraid of it and didn't want to be stalked by an arsonist. She took a deep breath. "They also didn't know about the connecting rooms. If I had been inside, and they started the fire, I may have been able to escape to your room."

"I agree, they did not know about our connecting rooms." He reached over to touch her arm. "I'm glad God was watching over us. Not only were we able to get away unscathed, but all the other room occupants are safe too."

"That is a blessing." She had to admit the fire could have been much worse. "If they had waited until the middle of the night . . ."

"But they didn't. And we're safe." He squeezed her arm, then released her. "We need to find another place to stay."

She tried not to sigh. "I hate the idea of putting others in harm's way."

"Your phone is back at the motel. I don't see how they can track you now."

"What about your phone?" She frowned, glancing over to see he was texting with someone, probably Mitch. "Anyone with the skills to track mine can track yours too."

"I know." His thumbs continued to work the phone. "That's why I'm following up with Mitch now, before I ditch it along the side of the road."

He was going to toss his phone? A flash of guilt hit hard in knowing Colin would be isolated from his family. The Finnegans had always been close, and not just while growing up. Rhy had followed up with Colin several times over the past—was it really only fifteen hours?

Faye tried to stay focused on driving despite having no clear destination in mind, other than getting far away from the fire at the motel. She was thankful Colin had managed to rouse everyone from their rooms. As terrible as it was to have this happen, his ability to preserve the lives of the guests was amazing.

Colin's bravery and determination to keep her safe were humbling. And he was right about God watching over them. She'd never felt His presence the way she had in every dangerous situation she'd found herself in. Willing her unruly stomach to settle down, she glanced at Colin, who was still texting with Mitch.

"Did Mitch give you any insight into what happened?"

"Not yet, he wants to look at the scene for himself before making a determination." Colin lifted his head from the phone. "He agrees it's possible that a delivery device was used to inject accelerant and fire into the room from the opening beneath the door."

She nodded and gestured toward the highway. "Do you care where we get the motel? There's a sign up ahead for the Weeping Willow Motel."

"Keep driving," he instructed. "I need to check in with Rhy before I get rid of my phone. We can always circle back to this place later. I don't want anything, even my phone, to connect us to the next place we choose to stay."

"Okay." She felt terrible about the money he was wasting in securing rooms at various motels and wished she had more cash on her. Whatever she'd had was back in the burning room. "If these guys can track our cell phones, shouldn't they have known the car sitting outside my room wasn't ours?"

"I thought of that, but they could have assumed we rented or borrowed a car from someone, the way we did." He shrugged. "They probably didn't take time to run the plates either. Why would they? They'd tracked your phone to the room, saw the vehicle, and started the fire."

"Yeah." She struggled to wrap her mind around it. "I'm surprised they weren't somewhere nearby, watching."

"They may have been, which is why we're getting a different vehicle as well as ditching my phone. I'm working out the logistics with Aiden. He has a friend who will swap vehicles with him. Aiden will then take Mitch's car to him and get a rideshare back to the homestead."

So much maneuvering and putting friends and family out by asking for help and she still didn't feel safe.

And doubted that would change until these guys were caught.

Her exhaustion from being up all night weighed heavily

on her shoulders. Her brief naps seemed like eons ago. Her goal had been to get back on a normal sleep schedule.

The arsonist made that difficult.

She continued heading south toward Milwaukee. It would be a good place to get rid of Colin's phone. Lots of hotels and motels there, which might help throw off her assailants.

"Hey, Rhy, I wanted to let you know that I'll be off-grid more than usual." Colin listened to whatever his brother said before responding. "I'm going to stop at a drugstore to get replacement phones, so I'll let you know my new number as soon as I have it."

Some drugstores were open twenty-four seven, but she wasn't aware of many that sold disposable phones. Not that she'd ever been in the market for such things. That was stuff that only happened in movies.

All of this was like something out of a movie. Normal people weren't targeted by arsonists.

As if killing her would make any difference in their miserable lives. None of it made any sense. Then again, neither of these former firefighters were thinking clearly. Their minds were clouded by resentment, anger, and a desperate thirst for revenge.

"Thanks, Rhy," Colin said, before ending the call. He glanced up. "Let's stop at the first twenty-four-hour drugstore you find."

"There's one up ahead. Although I don't know if they have phones."

"Some do, some don't." He sighed. "If we don't find one soon, we can wait until tomorrow. I would feel better having a replacement, though."

Considering how often they'd had to call 911, she felt the same way. Exiting the highway, she headed toward the advertised drugstore. Many places that used to be open all night long had changed their hours during the pandemic and had never gone back. It had been a roadblock they'd often talked about in the ED as they handed out prescriptions for patients. The hospital pharmacy couldn't provide prescriptions during the night because there were special regulations for outpatient pharmacies. They'd had to resort to giving one dose of medication in the ED, while hoping their patients could find an open pharmacy before needing the next dose.

She pulled into the parking lot of the pharmacy. There were other cars there, too, which was encouraging. Following Colin inside, she blinked at the extraordinarily bright lights.

Colin found the phones and paid for them in cash. Minutes later, they were back outside.

"If you don't mind, I'll drive from here." He held his hand out for the keys.

"Okay." She dropped the key fob into his hand, too tired to complain. She was too tired to do much of anything. Her physician brain understood the impact of an adrenaline rush and the resulting crash once the inciting event was over. She'd experienced the phenomenon often when they got word from the paramedic base about incoming gunshot wound victims. Multiple patients hitting their department at one time took a fair amount of coordination and collaboration. She wasn't a trauma surgeon, but she was still expected to help manage the influx of patients, prioritizing care for those injured the worst.

Understanding the physiology did not help battle the depths of her exhaustion now. She needed sleep, and soon.

"I'm going to head back toward the Weeping Willow

Motel," he said as he backed out of their parking spot. "That should work fine for what's left of the night."

She nodded, having nothing better to offer. There had been other motel signs, mostly from larger chains. Knowing Colin intended to pay in cash made the Weeping Willow a better option.

"Wait." She straightened in her seat. "What about your phone?"

"I have a plan." He flashed a reassuring smile and pulled into a gas station that was only a half mile from a small hotel. He slid out from behind the wheel and dropped his expensive cell phone on the ground. Without hesitation, he stomped on it with his heel, then tossed the broken remnants in the trash. "I'm hoping they think we're staying somewhere in this area, rather than going all the way back to the Weeping Willow. Aiden will be here shortly with our replacement vehicle."

"Okay." It didn't take too long for Aiden to arrive. He pulled up and parked alongside them.

Colin's brother had the red hair she remembered. He flashed her a warm smile as he handed over the keys to a Ford Explorer. "This belongs to a friend of mine, per your request. It was smart of you to grab the laptop, so make sure to take it with you. I'll handle returning Mitch's SUV."

"Thanks, bro," Colin said. "You're the best."

"I know," Aiden replied cheekily. Then his expression turned grim. "Seriously, stay safe, Colin. These guys aren't playing around."

"That's the plan." Colin clapped Aiden on the shoulder. "I'll get you and Rhy our new phone number as soon as I can get them powered up and activated."

"Understood. Take care." Aiden nodded at her, then took Colin's place behind the wheel of Mitch's SUV.

She climbed inside the Ford Explorer. Soon they were back on the road. Colin was doing everything possible to make sure they weren't followed. Dumping the phone here was a smart idea, yet deep down, she found herself hoping these guys didn't start recklessly setting multiple hotels on fire in a desperate attempt to find them. It would increase their chances of getting caught, but at this point, she wasn't about to put anything past them.

Faye closed her eyes, feeling sick at the thought, and lifted her heart in prayer. *Please, Lord Jesus, guide Mitch so he can find these guys before any innocent people are hurt!*

COLIN GLANCED AT FAYE. Her head rested on the passenger window, her eyes closed. He was glad she was getting some rest but hated to wake her once they'd reached their destination.

The near miss at the motel on the heels of the Molotov cocktail was troubling. Faye could have been seriously burned if she had entered her room rather than his. He wished he'd considered the possibility of her phone being tracked. Yet he still didn't understand how two firefighters had managed to do that. A former cop? Maybe, but firefighters didn't have the same sort of access to that level of information the way cops did.

Mitch needed to find out if they had cop connections that they weren't aware of. If not? He tried not to think about the possibility they were on the wrong track.

Battling fatigue, he turned one of the AC vents until there was cold air blowing directly on his face. That helped keep him sharp as he navigated the highway back toward the Weeping Willow Motel.

He noticed there were other signs for hotels too. He figured most of them didn't take cash, so he kept going. When they reached the Weeping Willow, he was relieved the vacancy sign was on.

After shutting off the vehicle, he noted Faye was still sleeping. He hurried inside, determined to get their rooms situated as quickly as possible.

It took a little sweet-talking and more cash, which Aiden had provided for him, to get two connecting rooms. He was glad to have them since that setup had helped save their lives.

Faye was still sleeping, so he drove to the last two rooms in the row and parked around the corner of the building. There were other cars, too, so he hoped their rooms would appear vacant to anyone driving past.

"Faye?" He patted her knee to get her attention. "Wake up. We're here."

"Huh?" She groaned and lifted her head, looking around in confusion. "Where?"

"The Weeping Willow. Come on, I'll help you get inside." He slid out and ran around to help take her hand, easing her from the passenger seat. She moved slowly, as if still half asleep, as they rounded the corner and headed toward the rooms. He glanced around and used the key to get inside.

The area appeared deserted, no noisy parties going on like the place they'd left. He steered Faye to the bed, then went over to unlock the connecting door. Glancing back at her, he asked, "Do you need help?"

"Huh?" She stared at him through the dim light filtering through the curtains. "Oh, no. I'm fine."

"Get some sleep." He left, giving her privacy, and made his way to the adjacent room. After unlocking the connecting door on his side, he left it open an inch. Just enough that she could easily get in if needed.

He desperately wanted to crawl into bed, too, but took the time to power up and activate their new phones. He quickly texted their new numbers to Rhy, Aiden, and Mitch so that they'd be able to reach either him or Faye as needed.

Then he sat for a minute, debating the wisdom of calling Chief Kimble. His boss would expect to be kept informed on what was happening. Yet, it was getting late, going on midnight.

Tomorrow. Scrubbing his hands over his face, Colin decided to wait until morning. Rest was a priority.

He couldn't protect Faye if he wasn't functioning at his best.

Sleep first, then more strategy in the morning. He doubted Mitch would have more information by then, but he and Faye needed a better plan. Something other than just staying hidden. It was obvious these disgraced fire-fighters wouldn't stop until they'd succeeded in their mission.

Or until Mitch found and arrested them.

Colin must have fallen asleep because a muffled thud woke him. He shot upright, straining to listen. Hearing only silence, he crept from the bed, taking a moment to grab the gun from the ankle holster Mitch had given him. Moving silently across the room, he stood to the side and peered through the narrow crack in the window.

There was no one outside that he could see. He relaxed, knowing the sound could have just been a car door closing. Then he heard a sob.

Faye?

He pulled the connecting door open and quickly crossed the threshold into her room. He held the gun with both hands, peering through the darkness. When he didn't see anyone in the room, he turned his attention to where Faye was crying on the bed.

"Faye? What's wrong? Are you okay?" He set the gun on the bedside table and sat beside her. She didn't seem to be aware of him. Was she dreaming? Based on everything that had transpired, he wouldn't be surprised if she were suffering a nightmare.

"Faye, wake up. You're safe, it's just a dream." He spoke louder and shook her shoulder. "Come on, wake up."

Her eyes opened, and she turned to stare at him. Then she relaxed and nodded. She wiped her eyes. "Sorry. I didn't mean to wake you."

"Nightmare?"

"Yes." She closed her eyes for a moment, then pushed upright to a sitting position. "I dreamed my father was dead."

"Oh, Faye." He gathered her close. "I'm sure your dad is fine. It was just a dream."

"I know." Her voice was muffled against his shirt. He'd slept in his clothes for modesty reasons, and so they could be ready to go at a moment's notice. "It was still awful."

"I'm sure it was." He stroked his hand down her back. The clock on the nightstand indicated it was five in the morning. Five hours of sleep wasn't much, but he felt refreshed, as if he'd gotten a solid eight hours of rest. "I planned to contact your father later this morning. You'll feel better if you talk to him too."

"Okay." She didn't move away but rested against him, as if she'd used up every ounce of her strength. Holding her was no hardship—except for remembering their incredible kiss, so he didn't mind.

After a few minutes, she lifted her head and once again

wiped at her face. Even with red and puffy eyes, she was beautiful. "Are you okay? Do you want me to get you some water?"

"I—yes, that would be good." She sniffled. "And a box of tissues."

He chuckled softly and ducked into the bathroom. He filled a glass with water and brought the box of tissues with him. She took them both gratefully, downing the water first, then blowing her nose. "I feel bad I woke you up."

"Please don't. I'm a very light sleeper." Years of working in a firehouse had him waking up at the drop of a hat. Which was strange because the snores from the other firefighter paramedics didn't bother him. Why a slight, unexpected sound caused him to jerk awake, he had no idea. He stood. "Try to get more sleep, okay? It's still early."

"Okay." She managed a smile. "It's really nice to know you're close by. I'm glad you insisted on sticking around."

"Anytime," he said, and he meant it. He liked Faye, a lot. More than a lot. But this wasn't the time or place to discuss his feelings. She needed him to keep her safe, not to kiss her again.

But maybe when this was over? Was it possible she'd be willing to see him again?

He turned toward the connecting door.

"Colin?"

He glanced back over his shoulder. "Yes?"

"Thank you."

"You're welcome. Good night." He forced a smile, slightly disappointed in her gratitude. He didn't want her feeling as if she owed him something. She didn't.

He was here because he liked her. And wanted to protect her. Maybe at first it was just because they'd grown up in the same neighborhood, attended the same high school, and her father was the fire chief. But that wasn't his motivation any longer.

He wouldn't leave her now, under any circumstances. Even if that meant losing his job. Which hopefully wouldn't happen.

Shaking off his concern, he crossed the threshold into his room.

Now that he was up, he figured sleep would be impossible. He made coffee in the small coffee maker included in their rooms, then slipped outside to grab the computer from the Explorer.

After booting it up, he used the free Wi-Fi offered by the motel to access the internet. He wasn't an expert in computer searches, but he knew how to access basic social media sites. He decided to start with Jayson Sanders to find police connections, then move onto Daniel Percy.

It was slow, painstaking work, giving him a new appreciation for not only the job Mitch had as an arson investigator, but what his brothers went through in their respective roles too. Rhy, Tarin, and Brady often lamented the never-ending paperwork required of them. Reports and more reports.

His paperwork at the firehouse was nothing in comparison. Sure, they had computerized forms to fill out when they did their paramedic runs, but they were nothing like this.

After working for an hour straight, Colin was no closer to coming up with a connection between the two firefighters and the police. At least, not from what he'd found on social media, but he had to admit, that may not mean much.

His brothers weren't active on social media. From what he heard, most cops weren't. They faced enough danger on the streets without giving people a direct link to them via one of these sites.

With a sigh, he closed the laptop and drained his coffee cup. He'd downed the whole pot and could easily drink another.

Was it too early to call Mitch? Probably.

He ducked into the bathroom to shower. When he emerged, he heard sounds of movement from Faye's room. He was making plans to head out for breakfast when his disposable phone chirped.

A text from Mitch. *Call me.*

He did so, staring forlornly at the empty coffeepot. Maybe he could sneak into Faye's room to grab hers to make more. "Hey, Mitch, what's up?"

"I just got raked over the coals because Chief Kimble hasn't been able to get a hold of you." The sound of crying in the background indicated Mitch was home with his kids. "Hey, Trina, it's okay. You're fine. She's walking," Mitch said to Colin. "But she can't do stairs. Thankfully, they're carpeted."

He knew Mitch had two kids, a little boy named Simon who was three and their youngest, Trina, was about eighteen months old. He didn't know much about kids, other than what he'd learned recently being around Brady and Grace's son, Caleb. He had no idea what age kids learned to walk up and down the stairs. "Sorry to hear the chief reamed you out."

"Yeah, I tried to assure him the best I could, but he wants to talk to you, Colin. And to his daughter."

"I planned to get in touch today, but it's barely six twenty in the morning. I figured I should at least wait until seven or so."

"Chief is up now, so don't wait," Mitch advised.

"Okay, I'll call him next. I've been thinking about how the two firefighters were able to track Faye's cell phone. I've been searching for any known connections with police, without success."

"I hate to tell you this, but we found Daniel Percy," Mitch said. "He's not our guy."

He frowned. "How can you be so sure?"

"Because he's dead." Mitch's tone was blunt. "Died from a self-inflicted gunshot wound to the temple."

The shocking news rocked him back on his heels. That was not at all what he'd expected. "What about his half brother, Jayson Sanders?"

"We're still searching for him," Mitch admitted. "The police finally spoke to another neighbor who saw him storing a suitcase in his car. He's still a suspect, but we may need to broaden our search now that we know the brothers aren't working together."

"Jayson threatened Chief Kimble," Colin felt compelled to point out.

"I know, that's why he's still on the list. But if he really did leave town, he'll have an ironclad alibi for these attempts."

Colin sank down onto the edge of the bed, knowing Mitch was right. Since yesterday, he'd been convinced that Jayson and Daniel had been working together to orchestrate these attacks.

If not them, then who? Who hated Faye enough to try to kill her?

CHAPTER TEN

Hearing the rumble of voices from Colin's room, Faye stepped through the connecting door, coffee cup in hand. Colin nodded at her as he finished up his call. "Thanks for the information, Mitch. Chief Kimble will be my next call. Stay in touch."

"What information?" She dropped down on the edge of the bed.

"Any chance you have more coffee?" Colin asked.

"I do." She went back to her room to fill a cup for him. He accepted it gratefully.

"Thanks." He took a sip, then added, "Daniel Percy was found dead from suicide."

"Suicide?" Stunned, she could only gape at him. "When? How?"

"Gunshot wound to the head, and not sure when. There's been no sign of Jayson, his half brother, yet either. Neighbor claims he left with a suitcase."

"Are you saying Mitch believes someone else is doing this?" She felt terrible knowing Daniel committed suicide. Not that she was responsible, but it was difficult to know he'd been depressed enough to do something so drastic. Behavioral health illnesses were difficult to diagnose, especially with the stigma attached to them. Men in particular were less likely to seek help for depression. Unfortunately, she'd taken care of many patients who'd attempted suicide, and the outcomes were not always good.

Like Daniel's.

"Jayson is still a suspect, he's the one who was fired recently and threatened your father." Colin held up his disposable phone. "Apparently, your dad is not happy with me. I'm calling him now."

"I'll talk to him." Faye sipped her coffee as Colin punched in her dad's phone number that he'd jotted down on the motel notepad. She thought he'd hand her the phone right off the bat so she could calm her dad down, but he didn't.

"Where have you been?" Her father's voice was so loud she could hear it too.

"I'm sorry, sir, but we've been flying under the radar after being found at our previous location." Colin didn't look fazed by her father's anger. "We had to leave in a hurry, and I needed to get rid of my phone."

"I want to talk to my daughter." His voice was still loud enough to hear.

"I understand, sir, but I want you to know Faye is safe." Colin handed her the phone without waiting for her father's response.

"Dad? I'm fine." She held Colin's gaze. "Thanks to Colin, I didn't get hurt in the last motel fire."

"I've been worried sick," her dad admitted. "Tell Colin I'm sorry I yelled, but he promised to keep me informed. I went a little crazy when I received no response to my text and phone messages."

"We don't have our phones anymore." She wasn't sure how much to tell him. Or how much Mitch had told him. "But I promise we're safe."

"Yeah, that's what I thought when you went to the last place," he groused. "Callahan better figure out who is behind these attacks, and quick."

"He's been working tirelessly to do just that, Dad." She didn't want her father to pressure Mitch any more than he already had. "Whoever is behind this has been relentless."

"I know, I know." He sighed. "It's not easy for me to sit back and wait, knowing you're the one in danger."

"But I have Colin protecting me, remember? He's a great guy. And I know Mitch will find the arsonist responsible for these fires."

"I have confidence in both Callahan and Finnegan." Her dad's tone had dropped several notches. "I feel better hearing your voice, Faye."

"I feel better after talking to you too." She smiled at Colin to reassure him the call was going well. "How is Annie? Still at her sleepover?"

"Yes, Claire spoke to her last night. She's fine. You're the one in danger here. I need you to stay in touch, understand?"

"Yes, Dad. I love you. Here's Colin." She handed the phone back.

"Sir? I take it Mitch filled you in on the latest attempt?" Colin asked. He listened for a minute, then nodded. "I hear you loud and clear. Hang on to this number, we'll call again later this afternoon or sooner if we learn anything new." Another pause, then, "Yes, sir. I promise."

"I'm sorry my dad was so rough on you." She grimaced as Colin set the phone aside. "Knowing these attempts are likely a way to get back at him has him more rattled than usual."

"I would feel the same way if my daughter was in danger." Colin tapped the computer. "I tried to find a connection between Jayson and Daniel to law enforcement but came up empty. Doesn't mean there isn't one."

"I can't believe Daniel is dead." She swallowed hard and set her empty coffee cup aside. The young man's suicide bothered her. "Do you think Jayson knows? Maybe that's why he packed up and left town."

"No idea." Colin sipped his coffee, his expression thoughtful. "Daniel and Jayson are friends on social media, but that doesn't necessarily mean they're close. Our theory was that they were working together, yet for all we know, they didn't talk much. Jayson is quite a bit older than Daniel, and they worked out of different firehouses."

"Does my father know?"

"Yes, Mitch filled him in." Colin rose to his feet. "Are you ready for breakfast?"

"You firefighters are obsessed with food," she teased.

"Hey, we eat when we can." Colin arched a brow. "I would think you would have the same approach considering your work is pretty much nonstop too."

"You're not wrong, but I make do with snacks in between patients." She stood and gestured to the door. "I'm ready if you are."

After tucking the computer case under his arm, he peered through the curtained window, then reached for the door. "We'll leave the keys here since we won't be back."

She removed the key from her pocket and dropped it on the table. Then followed him outside. Frowning, she asked, "Where's our car?"

"Around the corner." He glanced at her. "You don't remember?"

Now that he mentioned it, she did vaguely recall stumbling from a vehicle and crossing the parking lot while leaning heavily on him for support. "I guess I was pretty out of it, huh?"

"Understandable." He unlocked the Explorer and set the computer case in the back seat. "It was a long day."

That was putting it mildly. Still, he'd suffered the same long day considering they'd both worked night shift and had been together since seven thirty in the morning. Thankfully, getting sleep helped, and she felt almost normal as she climbed into the passenger seat.

"After we grab something to eat, we're going to meet up with Mitch in Milwaukee." He backed out of the parking lot and headed out onto the highway.

"Why are we meeting with Mitch? Does he have more questions for me?"

"No additional questions, but we need a plan. Hiding out indefinitely isn't going to work." He shrugged. "Your father is getting antsy, and frankly, so am I."

"My dad is fine." Or he would be, eventually. "I agree we should have a plan, though. Maybe we need to set up a trap to draw the arsonist out of hiding."

"I was thinking the same thing. Not that we would use you personally," he hastily added. "Your phone drew the arsonist out last night, we might be able to do something similar again, without you being anywhere nearby."

"I like that idea." She ignored the sliver of apprehension snaking down her spine as she considered the logistics. "I can easily buy a replacement phone from the same carrier as a way to draw the arsonist out. Do you think we also need to leak something to the press?"

"Not sure we need to go that far, but a replacement phone is a good place to start." He flashed a smile. "After breakfast."

She laughed. "Of course. I wouldn't dream of making you work hard on an empty stomach."

"I'm better with food in my belly." He glanced at the rearview mirror, then at her. "It's a beautiful day. I'm sure the lakefront is jammed with people. What would you normally do on your weekend off?"

She was embarrassed to tell him about her lack of social life. "Hard to remember what my life was like when I still had a house and a car. But normally, I'd get caught up on chores and take a long walk."

"You haven't dated since your divorce?"

"No time." It was a pathetic excuse, but she used it anyway. "The pandemic is over, but we still see patients suffering from COVID and the flu. Even in the summertime. And let's not forget the usual knife and gun club playing on the streets of the city. Spending time at home is about all I have the energy for these days."

"I'm sure it's been a rough few years," he agreed. "But you know time off is important. Everyone needs time off to recharge their batteries, to escape the rigors of the job. People like me need doctors like you to be well rested, happy, and healthy."

Since he was right, she nodded. "I know, and you're right. I'm overdue for a vacation, but I have time off scheduled in September."

"Me too." Colin grinned. "My brother Quinn is getting married."

"I'm happy for him."

"We are too. Quinn and Sami had some trouble in their

relationship, they were broken up for two years, but they're together now and happier than ever."

His comment made her think about her own wedding. There had been a time about three weeks before when she'd almost broken things off. Looking back, she'd instinctively known Rory wasn't right for her. Claire had told her she was just having the pre-wedding jitters that every bride experienced.

Somehow, she didn't think the Finnegan spouses-to-be experienced those same doubts.

She veered away from those thoughts. She wasn't in line to be the next Finnegan spouse. After the disaster with Rory, she'd vowed to never jump into marriage like that again. And the funny thing was, she'd known Rory for a year before they'd gotten married, never suspecting he was unfaithful.

Her career kept her busy enough. Too much time away from home had caused Rory to stray, or so he'd claimed.

"Are you familiar with Rosie's Diner?" Colin's question pulled her from her troubled thoughts.

"Yes, I've eaten there."

"Great. I love their pancake breakfast specials." He really was all about the food. "And Rosie always has fresh baked pastries too."

She could feel her hips widen just thinking about Rosie's pastries. But she nodded anyway. "Sounds good to me."

If not for the fact that they were on the road in some strange guy's car, with disposable cell phones and not one iota of luggage—unless you counted the laptop case—this was a pretty nice way to spend a Saturday morning.

An experience she longed to repeat once the danger was over.

FAR TOO AWARE of Faye sitting beside him, Colin forced himself to concentrate on the road, both the cars in front of him and those coming up from behind. He'd stayed in the right lane, driving barely five miles above the speed limit, forcing other travelers to pass him in their hurry to reach their destination.

So far, none of the cars had lingered behind him. Which had been the whole point. They weren't in a rush to reach Rosie's. He was hungry, but he knew Mitch needed time to investigate the possibility of setting a trap for the arsonist.

Mitch also wanted to meet with the detective who'd handled Daniel Percy's suicide. A note had been left behind, but the case would be thoroughly vetted to ensure this wasn't a homicide staged to look like a suicide.

Hard to believe Jayson would kill his own half brother, but hearing stories from his cop brothers, Colin knew anything was possible. Dysfunctional families had become a big draw in reality TV shows. First responders tended to see that dysfunction up close and personal.

And what his older siblings had experienced over the past eight months when their loved ones were in danger had been worse than anything portrayed on television.

He needed to call Rhy once he and Mitch came up with a plan. His brother would want to be apprised of the details. As a tactical expert, his brother's input would be invaluable in identifying any potential flaws in their plan too.

Yet Devon's pregnancy meant Rhy could not be involved at the scene. His oldest brother's place was at the homestead with his wife and unborn child. If Colin and

Mitch needed additional firearm support, he'd rather ask for Aiden's help.

The trip to Milwaukee proved uneventful. Which was a good thing as that meant their precautions regarding phones and swapping cars had worked. The parking lot at Rosie's was only half full, and he could see at least two empty tables as he drove by.

"Ready?" He stopped the Explorer and put the gearshift into park.

"Yep." Faye pushed open her door. "Do you need the laptop?"

He nodded and reached between the seats to snag it. "Mitch is meeting us here in about an hour."

Inside, he walked straight to the last booth along the line of windows. Rosie's Diner was an old-fashioned place, but the food was great, and he liked the quaint atmosphere. Rosie gave him a nod, indicating she'd be over shortly.

Faye peered at the plastic menu as he scanned the crowd. Rosie came over with two cups and a pot of coffee. "It's been a while, Colin. I've been worried you found a new hot breakfast spot."

"Never. You're my favorite, Rosie." He beamed at her.

"Ah, lad, you're always the sweet one, aren't you?" Rosie's thick Irish accent made him laugh. She'd been born in the States, just like he had been, but she liked to play up their Irish roots. "Slow down and enjoy your coffee. I'll be back to take your order."

"Wow, I didn't realize you were such a regular here," Faye teased.

The back of his neck went hot. "It's not that far from our firehouse. What can I say? I like the food, and Rosie is a gem."

"I see the pancake special, but that is an awful lot of food." She shook her head. "I'll stick with a veggie omelet."

"They're good too," he assured her. "I've had just about everything Rosie offers."

Once they'd placed their order, he savored his coffee. This had to be his last cup, he was already over his self-imposed limit. While they were waiting for their meals, Rosie brought over a large cranberry muffin.

"They're on special today," she said by way of explanation. He'd learned to never say no to Rosie's specials.

"Looks great, thanks," Colin said.

Rosie winked at him and gave them two small plates and two forks. "You need to share so you have room for breakfast."

Faye's brows hiked up, and she leaned over the table, keeping her voice low. "Does she always do this?"

"Petty much." He cut the muffin in half and put it on her plate. Then helped himself. "Don't argue until you've tried it."

To her credit, Faye took a bite. "Mmm, very good."

"Told you." He grinned and ate his portion. "Don't say no to Rosie."

When their meals arrived, he reached across the table to take Faye's hand. She didn't hesitate to clasp his fingers and bow her head. He was touched by the way she participated in his prayers.

"Lord, thank You for this wonderful meal You've provided for us. We also thank You for continuing to keep us safe in Your loving arms. Amen."

"Amen." Faye held his gaze for a long moment. "I hope whatever plan you and Mitch come up with keeps you safe, too, Colin. I don't want anything to happen to either of you. Or anyone else for that matter."

"Don't worry about us." He smiled and dug into his large pancake breakfast, complete with hash browns and bacon. When Rosie returned, he broke his rule about not having more coffee.

If he and Mitch were able to set up the plan he'd begun to formulate, this might be his last meal for a while. He knew better than to get his hopes up, but if planting Faye's phone to draw out the arsonist worked, they could have this case wrapped up by dinnertime.

And if it didn't work? He and Mitch would have to come up with a plan B.

As if on cue, his phone rang. Glancing at the screen, he confirmed the caller was Mitch. "Hey, we're in Milwaukee."

"Figured. Did you hit Rosie's?"

"Of course. Are you heading over to join us?"

"Soon. Give me about fifteen minutes. We're still checking Jayson Sanders's credit card purchases. So far he hasn't used it for anything. In my opinion, that's a big red flag. If this was some innocent vacation, he'd have charges pending."

"Does he use his card often?" Colin knew some people avoided credit cards, preferring to pay their way as they went along.

"Often enough up until three days ago. About the time the chief gave him the boot."

"Interesting. Okay, we'll wait for you here."

"See you soon." Mitch paused, then added, "And save some food for me."

"Ha ha. Later." He disconnected from the call.

"What's interesting?" Faye asked.

He explained about the lack of credit card charges for the past three days on Jayson Sanders's account. "Could be nothing. He may be cautious about spending since he's without a job."

"Sounds to me like he's hiding." She frowned. "What did you call it? Flying under the radar."

"Yeah, maybe. But not using a credit card isn't a crime." Suspicious? Yeah. But after learning of Daniel Percy's suicide, he thought it best not to jump to any conclusions. "How's your omelet?"

"Excellent. Much better than hospital food." She gave his plate a disparaging glance. "You're really going to eat all that?"

"Watch me."

By the time Mitch came in, a solid twenty minutes later, they had finished their meals. Mitch grimaced and said, "You didn't wait for me."

"Rosie knows you're coming," Colin assured him. Less than two minutes later, Rosie brought Mitch a cranberry muffin and coffee.

Once Mitch had placed his order, he turned the conversation to business. "I'm glad you're finished eating because I heard from the ME on the way over. He's working on the autopsy, cause of death is obviously the bullet wound in his temple, but we won't have the full tox screen for thirty days."

"Why so long?" Colin asked. "Can't he put a rush on it?"

"Toxicology screens take time," Faye said. "Especially in a case where they have no idea what, if anything, has been ingested."

"She's right," Mitch agreed. "Even with a rush on it, a month is the best they can do. I spoke to the detective who caught the case; it's your brother, Tarin."

Colin nodded. "What did Tare say?"

"He's being super cautious, unwilling to give his opinion one way or the other until all the forensics are back."

Again, Colin wasn't surprised. Tarin had made a call about a suicide five years ago that had ended up being a homicide. His brother wasn't about to make the same mistake again. "How long will that take?"

"At least until tomorrow, maybe Monday." Mitch sighed. "The only thing he would commit to is that the handwriting on the note looks to be a match to other documents found at the house. However, Tarin said Daniel could have written it under duress."

Great, so they basically knew nothing more than they had earlier that morning. "Okay, I guess we'll have to wait to see what Tarin comes up with."

"Yeah. Between that and the lack of credit card charges, we don't have much to work with." Mitch eyed him over the rim of his cup. "You mentioned setting a trap for this guy. I have to tell you, Chief Kimble isn't on board with that idea."

Colin frowned. "Did you assure him this trap would not place Faye in harm's way? That we don't have many options to find this guy unless we do something significant to draw him out?"

"I did." Mitch glanced over at Faye seated beside him. "You may need to call your dad again. I think my bringing up the plan rattled him."

"I will, but I agree with Colin." She stared into her empty coffee cup. "We need to do something. How much longer does he think we should sit around and wait for someone to find this guy?"

Mitch lifted his hands in surrender. "Hey, don't shoot the messenger. I'm on your side."

Colin wished Mitch hadn't broached the chief until

they had nailed down a possible plan. He leaned forward, propping his elbows on the table. "First, we need to stop at a phone store and get a replacement for the one Faye left behind in the motel. Then we need to head over to the American Lodge to talk to Gary."

Mitch nodded slowly. "You're thinking Gary can set up a decoy room with Faye's phone to draw the arsonist out of hiding."

"Exactly." His brother Rhy had tried something similar several months ago when his wife Devon had been in harm's way. Devon hadn't been his wife at the time, but that hadn't stopped his brother from putting his life on the line for her. And now they were married and expecting their first child together. God worked in mysterious ways.

"That might work," Mitch said.

"Gary installed security cameras outside the motel. Rhy saw them back in January when he tried to set a trap there."

"What happened?" Faye asked. "Did the ruse work?"

"The guy Rhy was trying to draw out saw the cameras and took off." He shrugged. "So no, it didn't work. The same thing could happen this time too. Unless we can come up with a way to hide the cameras to avoid detection."

"Security cameras, huh?" Mitch pondered that for a moment. "I like it, Colin. And I know Gary pretty well. He'll jump at the chance to help us catch this guy."

"If he has any empty rooms to spare. It's summer, and a weekend too." Colin shrugged. "We might have to wait until Sunday night, but I figure it's worth a trip over there to talk to him. The sooner we come up with a plan, the sooner we can set it up."

"But where am I going to be while this trap is set?" Faye asked.

He hesitated, knowing she wouldn't like it. "You'll need

to stay with your dad and Claire in Brookland, Faye. Leave the American Lodge to me, Mitch, and Aiden."

She frowned. "I don't like that idea."

He'd known she wouldn't, but that was too darn bad. Because he made a promise to her father to keep her safe.

And he wasn't about to break that vow.

CHAPTER ELEVEN

"The reason I haven't gone to my father's house since this nightmare began is because I don't want to put his wife or my sister in danger. That hasn't changed." Faye tilted her chin stubbornly. "I'm sure you and Mitch can figure out some way to have me be in the room too."

"Not happening." Colin's tone was firm.

"She has a point about the danger to the chief's wife and daughter," Mitch said. "We can keep her someplace else, like another motel."

"I'd rather her dad be the one to watch over her." Colin sighed and rubbed the blond stubble on his jaw. Normally, he was clean-shaven, but they'd been in various motels now, without a razor. "I could see if Rhy can get someone from his team to watch her for us rather than her dad."

"I'm not helpless." The words came out sharper than she had intended. She tried to soften them. "I know I'm not a cop, but with you guys watching the motel, I think it's best if I stay inside the room with my phone. If the arsonist doesn't see me going inside, he may view it as a trap. Especially if he knows Gary is a retired firefighter. That alone may cause him to be suspicious."

There was a long moment of silence as Colin stared at her. She could tell he didn't like it, but he was considering the possibility of failure if they didn't include her.

"Please, Colin." She rested her hand on his arm. "Let me do my part to help catch this guy."

"She's right about the possibility of the arsonist knowing Gary," Mitch said. "If he's at all associated with the fire department, he'll know Gary would support us in a time of need. Yet, that could work in our favor too. Especially if we make it clear Faye is inside the room and make a show of leaving her behind. That may be enough to draw him out of hiding, goading him into trying again."

Colin remained silent, sipping his coffee. Finally, he sighed and glanced pointedly at Faye. "Fine. We'll do it your way. But I'm staying in the room with you."

"Okay, whatever you think is best." She wasn't going to argue.

"It would make the setup more believable," Mitch agreed. "You still have my backup piece?"

"Yes." Colin's expression was grim. "And I won't hesitate to use it."

"Okay, then give me some time to get in touch with Gary." Mitch wiped his face with his napkin. "As you said, he may not have a room until tomorrow night or Monday."

"I have to work on Monday," Faye reminded Colin. "You're on duty too."

"I know. We'll see how it goes." He didn't smile, clearly still not happy with her. "I would like to find this guy sooner rather than later."

She looked away, shrugging off his annoyance. She was the one in danger. For whatever reason, the arsonist had fixated on her. Better her than her sister, Annie. At sixteen, her sister wouldn't be able to protect herself.

Making a mental note to follow up with her father later, to ensure her sister was still safe, she finished her coffee. Colin and Mitch were ready to leave too.

"You'll let us know what Gary says?" Colin asked as they stood.

"Of course. Where are you spending the day?" Mitch glanced between her and Colin. "Another motel?"

She wrinkled her nose at the thought. "We need to replace my phone first. After that, maybe we can head to a park. Or hang out at the lakefront for a bit. I'm kinda sick of motel rooms."

"We'll see." Colin's expression was noncommittal. "Take care, Mitch. I hope Gary can make this work."

"And if not?" Faye asked. "Can't we just choose another motel?"

"Maybe." Colin grimaced. "I hate the idea of putting anyone else in danger, though. Gary's place would be perfect."

"It'll work out, you'll see." Mitch clapped him on the back as they walked outside. "Have faith, cousin."

That made Colin smile. "You know I do."

"Good. Later, Colin. Faye." Mitch nodded at each of them and headed for his vehicle, leaving them alone.

Colin wordlessly turned toward their borrowed vehicle. She followed, swallowing the urge to apologize. Especially since she wasn't sorry for sticking up for herself. She only regretted making him angry.

Not that she controlled his emotions. He wanted to protect her just as much as she wanted to protect her family.

She jumped into the passenger seat, keenly aware of

Colin beside her. He started the car, then turned to face her. "I promised your father I'd keep you safe. You're making that incredibly difficult."

"I know, but you have kept that promise." She took his hand. "I will assure my dad that this is my decision."

"Yeah." He sighed heavily, staring down at their entwined fingers. "That only works if we make it out of this unscathed."

"We will." She managed a smile. "You have faith that God is watching over us, right? I do too."

He surprised her by lifting her hand and kissing her fingers, then letting her go. "Okay, time to hit the road."

After leaving Rosie's, Colin headed to the freeway. She was surprised by the amount of traffic along both sides of the highway, people heading to summer lake houses and cabins to spend quality time with their families over the weekend.

Something she hadn't experienced personally in a long time. But she knew her dad had taken Claire and Annie to a nice lake home for several weeks over the summer months. The realization had her straightening in her seat. "Colin, I have an idea."

"Yeah?" He glanced at her. "You've changed your mind about going to your dad's house while we spring the trap?"

"No. I don't know why this didn't occur to me earlier, but my dad rents a lake house for the entire summer. They don't stay there the whole time, of course, but often enough. I think we should set up the trap there."

"What sort of summer lake house?" Colin asked. "You didn't mention it earlier."

"I know, I'm an idiot." She shook her head. "I rarely go there, that's why it didn't occur to me before now." She didn't add that the lake house was something her father did for his new family, not his old one. Irritated with her petty thoughts, she shook them off. "My schedule makes it hard to get away in the summer, but I was there over Memorial Day about two years ago, I think? I'm sure I can find it again."

"You remember the address?"

"It's on Fish Lake in Wautoma, Wisconsin. I tend to have a pretty good memory." It was almost photographic, but not exactly. Her gifted memory had been an asset in getting through medical school. "I know the cabin is roughly two hours away, maybe longer with traffic. I wish I'd remembered this earlier. The good news is that if the American Lodge is full, we can use the cabin as plan B."

"Are there security cameras?" Colin asked.

"No." She shrugged. "But the house overlooks the lake, so someone coming by car or foot would approach from the rear of the property. There's not any woods close to the house either; my stepmother doesn't like bugs."

He nodded slowly. "Okay, that's helpful. We'll see what Mitch comes up with. If nothing else, we can use the place as a temporary hideout until it's time to spring the trap."

"I really wish I'd thought of it earlier." She could blame the stress of being on the run and the lack of sleep, but the truth was, she didn't consider the lake house hers. Her father had offered the place to her whenever she wanted to come up, but a narrow glance from Claire had confirmed her stepmother hadn't liked that idea.

And really, driving all the way up to the lake house by herself didn't hold much appeal. The one time she'd gone up two years ago, the experience had proved to be somewhat awkward, so she'd stayed away, using work as an excuse.

"We need to get your replacement phone," Colin said, changing the subject. "Any particular place you shop?"

"Yes. I use the store at Mayfair Mall."

"Great. We'll head there first. And we can pick up a few items of clothing if you'd like too."

She looked down at her wrinkled navy-blue capri pants and her blue and green top. A change of clothing would be nice, but it wasn't imperative. "I thought we weren't going to use our credit cards?"

"We can for now, temporarily." He put a hand on her knee. "This way, our arsonist will know we're back in town and shopping. He won't be surprised when your phone is back online."

"Makes sense." She tried not to show her concern. This guy had tracked her down to the park outside the courthouse, attempting to burn her with blatant disregard for the innocent lives he put in harm's way.

She trusted Colin and Mitch. They were being strategic about drawing the arsonist out of hiding. Overall, she liked the plan. The sooner they knew who this guy was, the better.

Even though getting him behind bars would bring an end to her time with Colin. She told herself that was okay. She had to deal with the insurance company about her house and car anyway. No doubt working with claims adjusters and contractors to oversee the repairs to her home.

Since those thoughts were downright depressing, she decided to focus on the present. Colin pulled into the parking lot of the mall. They parked, then walked to the closest entrance.

"It's to the right," she said as they entered the cool air conditioning.

"I see it. We'll get the phone first, then pick up some clothes." He glanced down at his jeans. "Aiden is shorter than I am. I feel like people are staring."

She scoffed. "If they are, it's because you're good-looking, not the clothes themselves."

"You think I'm good-looking?" His smile widened.

She shook her head in feigned disgust. "There isn't a single bad-looking Finnegan, so don't pretend I'm the first to mention it."

"You're the only one that matters." His tone wasn't light and teasing anymore, but she reminded herself not to make too much of it.

Brushing past him, she approached the open counter. Getting the cell phone replaced took longer than she liked, mostly because the guy kept trying to upsell devices and accessories.

"I just want the phone and plan I had, thank you," she said firmly.

Once she'd purchased the new phone and logged into her account to transfer all her contacts and information, she tucked the phone into her pocket and turned away. "I'm ready."

"No problem." Colin accompanied her out of the store. "Where to first?"

Shopping with him seemed a bit personal. They hit a women's clothing store first, then another store for him. Soon they were carrying several shopping bags back out to the car. He'd just stored them in the back when his phone rang.

"It's Mitch." He slammed the back hatch, then answered the phone. "Hey, Mitch. I have you on speaker. Did you talk to Gary?"

"Bad news, he has no rooms open tonight. But he does have one room opening on Sunday night. I told him we'd take it."

"I figured it was a long shot given the tourist season,"

Colin admitted. He met her gaze. "We have a replacement phone for Faye. She mentioned Chief Kimble has a lake house in Wautoma that he rents for the entire summer. I think we're going to head there for the night."

"She just thought of this now?" Mitch asked.

She flushed. "Yes, I'm sorry about that. I have only been there once, and that was over two years ago. I don't think of it as my place and haven't been there in so long, so it never occurred to me to use it as a safe house."

"Well, better late than never," Mitch drawled. "Seriously, Faye, it's okay. I understand."

"We will need to turn off Faye's new phone until tomorrow," Colin said. "I don't like it, as this guy could sense a trap, but we can set that up too. Maybe have Faye make a call to her father as a reason to turn it back on."

"That should work." Mitch was silent for a moment. "Faye, your dad only rents the place, right? He's not an owner?"

"That's correct," Faye confirmed. "He only rents. Doesn't want the hassle of owning the place year-round."

"Okay, that helps. The arsonist has been able to track you up until you lost your phone, so I'm encouraged that's how he's been finding you. Property ownership is easy to find online; it's not confidential. A rental agreement would be much harder to uncover."

"I agree," Colin said. "There's no way any of the guys in the various firehouses could know about this. It's not as if they talk to the chief about his personal life."

"Right. However, I'm a little concerned with you guys being up there alone," Mitch said. "Do you want me or one of my brothers to head up there to help watch the place?"

"Not your brothers, you all have families," Colin protested. "I'll see if Aiden can lend a hand. He's single and not currently deployed. Besides, as long as Faye's phone is off, I think we're fine. So far we haven't been found since the phone was left at the motel."

"The one that almost burned down," Mitch pointed out. "Yeah, okay. It's better if I stay here working the case anyway. We're still trying to track down Jayson Sanders. If I can find him, this entire plan may be a moot point."

"That would be great if you could find him," Colin said. "Don't worry about us. We'll be safe at the lake house."

"Okay. Stay in touch."

"You too." Colin disconnected from the line. He opened the driver's side door. "Ready to go?"

"Yes." She slid into the passenger seat and made sure to shut down her brand-new replacement phone before clicking her seat belt on. Ignoring the shiver of apprehension, she gave Colin directions on how to get to Wautoma.

It would be strange to be there alone, without her dad or stepmother. Claire would be upset if she knew, but since Claire and Annie were in Brookland, the infringement on their privacy shouldn't matter.

Still, the tingle of unease wouldn't leave her alone.

FAYE'S DIRECTIONS WERE SPOT-ON, as if she were some sort of human GPS. The thought made him smile.

The trip passed uneventfully, although the congested traffic had added a good thirty minutes to their time.

"How long before Aiden gets here?" Faye asked.

"He's probably twenty minutes behind us." He wondered if she didn't like the idea of being there with him alone. Pulling into the driveway, he was impressed with the size of the house. "Wow, this is bigger than I expected."

"Yeah, well, only the best for Claire." She winced, then added, "Sorry, I didn't mean to sound like sour grapes. My dad has worked hard his entire life and loves spending time here. He deserves it, and so does Claire."

He nodded, reading between the lines. This was her dad and Claire's place. Not hers. "I get it, with our schedules, it's difficult to get time away."

"Yes, exactly." She looked relieved he didn't press the issue.

"I assume you have a key to get in?" He pulled up to the garage door.

"There's a key code." She pushed out of the SUV and walked to the garage. A moment later, the door opened. The interior was clean and empty, looking as if it wasn't used very often.

He was a little surprised Chief Kimble didn't get up here more, but Faye's comment about Claire not liking bugs made it sound like her dad would be here if he could. He pulled the SUV into the garage, then got out. He grabbed their shopping bags, while Faye entered a key code into the lock on the garage door.

It was reassuring to see two sets of locks. "Do you mind giving me the code?"

Glancing over her shoulder, she rattled off the four-digit number. Committing it to memory, he followed her inside, gazing at the spacious kitchen. It was beautifully done with granite counters and white cabinets. The stainless-steel appliances appeared to be brand new.

"Very nice," he commented, carrying the shopping bags through the area.

"Yes, it's no hardship to stay here." Her tone was light, devoid of the earlier sarcasm. "The master bedroom is down here, but there are two others upstairs. We can take those if you like."

"It may be better if you sleep in the master, and I take the sofa." No way did he want to be trapped on the second floor in the event of a fire. Not that he expected the arsonist to show up here, but it was always better to be prepared.

"That's fine. There's a guest bathroom down here you can use. Obviously, there's also one in the master suite."

"That works perfect. I'll put my clothes in the guest bathroom." He rummaged inside to remove the items he'd purchased, then handed the shopping bag to her. "The rest are yours."

"Thank you." She slipped down the hall into the master suite.

He showered, shaved, and changed into fresh clothing. Feeling better, he went to the kitchen to rummage in the fridge. Not much in there other than a few bottles of water and an assortment of condiments. Turning his attention to the freezer, he found some frozen ground beef. He pulled it out, figuring he'd grill hamburgers for dinner.

Since Faye was still in the master suite, he poked around the rest of the property. The view of the lake was stunning, and there were many boats on the water. He noticed there was a speedboat suspended in a lift on the pier below. The boat was likely included in the rental property.

The area all around the house was clear of trees and brush. Made it more difficult for someone to sneak up on the place. He went outside to walk the perimeter. Motion sensor lights popped on as he walked by. *Even better*, he thought with satisfaction. The only safety feature they were missing were security cameras, but he'd take what he could get.

Curious, he walked all the way down to the lake. He had to admit, this was a nice setup. One thing for sure, if the Finnegans were renting this place for the summer, the property wouldn't be sitting empty. There would be family members coming and going just about every week as their schedules allowed.

Turning from the stunning view, he headed back up the gentle slope to the house. He keyed in the code she'd provided to gain access through the main door. When he caught a glimpse of Faye, his heart thudded in his chest, and his mouth went dry. It took him a few minutes to force himself to step forward.

She was beautiful. Her dark hair appeared to be freshly washed and dried, left down in wavy strands to her shoulders. She wore a pair of formfitting ankle-length jeans that hugged her curves, along with a dark-blue T-shirt. The clothes might be casual, but to him, they only added to her attractiveness.

Get a grip, Finnegan, he silently warned. *This is not a romantic weekend getaway.*

The lake house made it difficult to remember they were hiding from the arsonist, staying off-grid until they could set their trap at the American Lodge.

"I—uh," he stumbled over his words. "I pulled ground meat from the freezer. I don't think your dad will mind if we grill burgers."

"No, of course not." Her smile didn't quite reach her eyes. "He told me to come here any time and to help myself."

"He did?" That surprised him, given the fact she hadn't been here in two years.

She shrugged and turned away. "Claire didn't like it, so I never took him up on his offer. But I highly doubt he'll notice a missing package of frozen ground beef."

"Okay." He watched as she stared out at the lake for a long moment. "Faye, are you all right with this plan? If you don't want to stay here, we can find someplace else to go."

"That's not necessary," she hastened to reassure him. "Silly to have you spend money on another motel when we can stay here for free. I wish I'd thought of it sooner."

He crossed over to stand beside her. "This is about your stepmother, isn't it?"

She flushed. "It's silly."

"Not if it's bothering you."

She blew out a breath and turned to lean back against the granite counter. "Claire isn't my mother, and to her credit, she never tried to be. She's a nice lady and makes my dad happy, which is important. I wouldn't want my dad to grieve forever or choose to live the rest of his life alone. I'm truly thrilled they have each other."

He could tell she was being completely honest. To a point. "But," he prompted.

"But she is really focused on her family. I—tend to be an afterthought." She grimaced. "That makes me sound like I'm twelve and jealous. I'm not. But I'm also not comfortable around her for an extended length of time. Spending the Memorial Day weekend here with them was two days too long. Holidays are about all I can handle."

"I see." And he did. "You must miss being part of the family."

She nodded slowly, grief shadowing her blue eyes. "Yes. I dearly miss the family I had. I miss my mom every day."

"I miss my parents too."

"I know, and what you went through was even worse, Colin. At least I still have my dad."

"You can't compare your grief to mine; it's not a contest. I have my family, and Rhy was phenomenal in keeping the siblings together."

"He was." Her smile was sad. "I know my dad was very impressed with the way Rhy and Tarin stepped up."

"That's nice to hear." He'd idolized her dad back then and had nothing but respect for him now. "And I want you to know I'm here for you, Faye. Any time you need me."

She dropped her gaze to the floor. "That's very sweet. You're the nicest guy I've ever met."

He didn't necessarily want to be the nicest guy, he wanted more. Her sadness tugged at his heart, and he couldn't help pulling her into his arms. The fact that she moved toward him, wrapping her arms around his waist, gave him a secret thrill.

"I'm here," he repeated, whispering in her ear. "I care about you."

She didn't answer, which made him wonder if he'd stepped too far over the line. He was about to apologize when she pulled away, just far enough to kiss him.

Heat flared as he deepened their kiss. He'd always admired her smart mind and dedication to caring for patients. Getting to know her these past couple of days only deepened his feelings for her.

The sound of a car door slamming shut had them jumping apart. Dazed, he glanced toward the door facing the road. He caught a glimpse of Aiden's truck in the driveway.

"Um, my brother is here." His brain was still foggy from the impact of their kiss. He did his best to clear his mind as he made his way to the door.

While wishing Aiden had taken longer to get here.

Much longer.

CHAPTER TWELVE

Wow. Just . . .wow.

Her knees weak, Faye leaned back against the counter for support. She'd thought Colin's first kiss was amazing. This one had been ten times better. She pressed a hand to the center of her chest, willing her thudding heart to settle down.

She wasn't sure why his kiss had provided such an impact. She'd been married. Now divorced. Yet she could say with complete honesty that Rory's kiss had never made her feel like this.

More proof she'd rushed into marriage with the wrong guy.

Colin greeted his brother as if nothing had happened between them. Maybe he hadn't been knocked off balance the way she had. She listened as he explained the key code on all the entrances before leading his brother inside.

"Hi, Aiden." She was relieved her voice sounded steady. "It's nice of you to come."

"Not a problem." Aiden smiled. "I've been gone a lot

lately, so I've missed out on most of the fun my older siblings have had."

"Fun?" Colin shook his head. "They've all barely managed to escape with their lives."

"What do you mean?" She frowned, glancing between the two brothers. "They were all in danger?"

"Yeah." Colin shrugged. "Mostly because the women they were determined to protect were in harm's way."

"Don't forget how Brady's son, Caleb, was kidnapped," Aiden said. "That hit close to home."

"Kidnapped?" She couldn't even imagine. "That's awful."

"Caleb is fine," Colin hastened to reassure her. "Brady and Grace are happily married now too."

"Better watch out, bro," Aiden teased, lightly punching Colin in the shoulder. "You're next."

"Knock it off," Colin muttered, the tips of his ears turning red. "You're embarrassing Faye."

"Not my intention," Aiden said by way of apology.

"It's fine." She hoped her face wasn't as flushed as Colin's ears.

"Where do you want me to drop my duffel?" Aiden asked, thankfully changing the subject.

"Pick one of the two bedrooms upstairs," Colin said. "I was planning to sleep on the sofa."

"We should take turns keeping watch." All sense of joking had vanished from Aiden's tone. "Three- or four-hour shifts should do the trick."

"Yeah, okay." Colin gestured toward the patio doors overlooking the lake. "We have water behind us, not that the arsonist couldn't show up by boat. If the guy even knows where we are, which is unlikely."

"Agreed." Aiden glanced around the house with frank

admiration in his gaze. "Nice place. You must love spending time up here."

She nodded, unwilling to get into her family dysfunction. "My dad rents it every summer. The owner is a hunter and tends to come up during the fall. I guess the summer rental income pays the mortgage and property taxes."

"Think of the family parties we could have here." Aiden elbowed Colin in the ribs. "Rhy is always talking about taking the family to Ireland, but this would be cheaper, especially since the family is growing by the minute."

Faye was struck by how Aiden saw the house and immediately thought of spending time here with the Finnegan family. So different from her stepmother.

"I'm sure this place isn't cheap, so you may as well stop planning our next year's summer vacation." Colin gestured to the front door. "Let's head outside to walk the property before we make dinner. I want you to see the layout and the placement of each motion detection light. Having security cameras would be better, but this setup isn't bad."

"Sounds good." Aiden flashed a quick smile in her direction before following his brother outside.

Faye took the time alone to pull herself together. It was probably a good thing Aiden had come to lend moral and backup support. Not that she didn't trust Colin to remain in control, because she did. He was too honorable to take advantage of the situation.

No, it was her own erratic emotions she needed to worry about. She couldn't lie to herself, she desperately longed to kiss him again.

But that couldn't happen. She needed to remember this was a temporary situation. As much as she liked and trusted Colin, she really wasn't interested in planning a future.

She'd already made one huge mistake. The last thing she intended to do was to jump into another relationship.

Her long hours at the hospital were a big part of the reason Rory had cheated. That part of her job wouldn't change. Colin worked a different schedule, too, but he would also have several days off while she was working.

Colin wouldn't cheat, of that she felt certain. But that didn't mean a relationship would be easy. No, she didn't want to risk being hurt like that again.

She pushed away from the counter and searched the kitchen for something to accompany their hamburger meal. She found a box of French onion mix and set that aside. In the freezer, she found a pack of four corn on the cobs wrapped together, so she pulled those out too.

Maybe not the healthiest meal on the planet, but tasty. Colin and Aiden were both lean and muscular, making her self-conscious about the few added pounds she carried.

No more stress eating at work, she silently admonished. It wasn't easy to get into a regular exercise routine with her long shifts, but she made a mental note to do better.

The ground beef was still frozen. She was debating defrosting it in the microwave when Colin and Aiden returned.

"Oh, hey. I'll take care of dinner." Colin took the frozen meat from her hands. "You just rest and relax."

"What, you don't trust me?" She lifted a brow.

"Colin is proud of his culinary skills," Aiden said dryly. "He wants to show off for you."

"That's not it at all, I want her to rest," Colin corrected. He nodded at the corn. "Are you sure your dad won't mind if we eat that?"

"Of course not. Everything here is fair game," she said. "Honestly, I'm sure he'll be relieved. Claire buys tons of food, then eats like a bird. I heard him complaining about it because they end up tossing a lot of food at the end of summer."

"What?" Aiden's eyes widened in horror. "That's horrible. That would never happen at the homestead."

"Because we all eat like bears coming out of hibernation," Colin agreed.

"True." Aiden grinned. "Remember when I stabbed my fork into the back of your hand?"

"You mean at Thanksgiving last year when we were fighting over the drumstick? How could I forget?" Colin shook his head. "You're lucky you didn't injure any of the tendons along the back of my hand."

"You made such a big deal out of a little blood." Aiden snickered. "Four little holes, you were fine."

Faye glanced between the brothers, not sure if they were kidding.

"I might still have scars." Colin made a show of inspecting the back of his hand.

"Doubtful." Aiden reached for his duffel. "I'll take this upstairs. Let me know when dinner is ready."

"You're not going to help?" Colin asked as if in protest.

"It's not a four-course gourmet meal, is it? What do you need help with?" Aiden turned and headed to the second floor.

Faye was tempted to call Aiden back but held her tongue. Colin busied himself with defrosting the hamburger meat while she took a seat at the kitchen table.

"He really stabbed the back of your hand with a fork?"

"Yep." Colin arched a brow. "You would think Rhy and Tarin would have stuck up for me, but all they did was laugh."

"You guys have a funny way of getting along." She

couldn't imagine doing anything like that to Annie. And if she had? Claire would have hit the ceiling.

"Hey, laughter is the best medicine, right?" He shrugged. "No matter how mercilessly we tease each other, I know every single one of my siblings would walk through fire for me if necessary."

"That must be nice." She could not say the same; although in truth, Annie was too young for them to have established a close relationship. Annie adored their father, though, so in that respect, she suspected her half sister would do anything to protect him.

"Anything I can do to help?" She made the offer, despite seeing for herself that he had everything under control.

"Nope. I noticed there's a gas grill outside." He grimaced. "It will work, although I prefer the old-fashioned method of using charcoal."

"Because firefighters like to play with fire?"

His grin widened. "Sometimes."

She chuckled. "There's an area outside where we could build a bonfire."

"I saw that and would love nothing more. Unfortunately, that's out of the question for tonight." His brown gaze turned serious. "We'll need to stay inside just to be safe."

She nodded, masking her disappointment. Rising to her feet, she headed for the master suite. It was strange to be staying in there, but she did her best to shake off the apprehension. She'd decided to sleep on top of the bedspread, using a light blanket for cover.

Besides, it wasn't likely she'd get much sleep. Not while knowing both Colin and Aiden would be staying up to guard the place.

Twenty minutes later, Colin shouted, "Dinner's ready!"

She hurried out to the kitchen, listening as Aiden pounded down the stairs.

"It's about time. I'm hungry." Aiden rubbed his stomach. "You're the best cook behind Devon and Elly."

"Thanks, I think." Colin set the grilled corn and large juicy burgers on the table. "We don't have buns, but this will have to do."

"Looks delicious, thanks." Faye dropped into the chair beside Colin.

"I'll say grace." Colin took her hand in his. Aiden clasped his hands together and bowed his head. This was clearly a family tradition. "Lord Jesus, we thank You for this food we are about to eat. We ask that You continue to keep us all safe in Your care. And that You guide us to the truth. Amen."

"Amen," Aiden echoed.

"Amen," Faye agreed.

"Dig in!" Aiden reached for a grilled ear of corn.

Colin lightly smacked his hand. "Ladies first. And this is her family's food, so be nice."

"You're just getting back at me for the fork incident," Aiden groused. But then he grinned. "Help yourself, Faye."

She did, then smiled as the two Finnegans fought over the extra burger and ear of corn. In the end, they didn't resort to hand stabbing but split the burger and corn cob in half.

Watching them made her wish she had a closer relationship with Annie. Something she silently promised to work on once this nightmare was over. Just because Annie was fourteen years younger didn't mean they couldn't spend girl time together. Maybe do a spa day or go shopping.

The Finnegans were an in-your-face reminder that

family was important. And if she were honest, it was time for her to do her part with Annie and Claire.

AS MUCH AS he appreciated his brother's willingness to back him up, Colin wished he had more time alone with Faye. Which probably wasn't smart. He needed to remain focused on the threat posed by the arsonist.

When they finished their meal, Faye insisted on washing the dishes. Since he and Aiden needed to work out their guard duty schedule, he gestured for his brother to follow him into the living room.

"You want first watch?" Colin asked.

"You tell me what's better for you," Aiden countered. "I'm well rested, so you can get some sleep first if you'd like."

He nodded slowly. "That's probably for the best. Thanks. If you can give me four hours, that would be great."

"Not a problem." Aiden grinned. "How are things going between you and the pretty doc? I'm seeing sparks when you look at each other." He wiggled his eyebrows suggestively.

Scowling, he shook his head. "Don't, Aiden. She's going through a rough time. Tease me all you like but leave Faye alone. She's not used to siblings jabbing at each other."

"Ah, so it's like that, is it?" Aiden adopted a fake Irish accent. "Me thinks you protest too much."

He rolled his eyes. "And I think you have too much time on your hands." He stood and stretched. "Behave and wake me up earlier if you need to."

"I'll be fine, lad," he said with the same fake Irish accent. Truthfully, Aiden had the accent nailed, but he wasn't about to encourage him. "Don't you worry, the lass will be fine under my protection."

"You're an idiot," he said without heat.

"Hey, I almost forgot." The fake Irish accent was gone now. "I brought a spare gun from Rhy's safe."

"Oh, that's okay. Mitch Callahan gave me his backup weapon." He bent and unbuckled the ankle holster, showing his younger brother the weapon. "I haven't needed it, thankfully."

"That is a good thing," Aiden agreed. "Glad you have something to use if needed."

"I do. Good night." The hour was early, barely seven forty, but since he planned to be awake between midnight and four in the morning, he'd do his best to sleep. The good thing about working as a paramedic firefighter was that he'd trained himself to sleep between calls. This shouldn't be any different.

Except, it was. Only because he could still smell the flowery scent that clung to his clothes after holding Faye in his arms. He shifted restlessly, doing his best to focus on prayer, the way he usually did when needing to fall asleep quickly.

The next thing Colin knew, Aiden was shaking his shoulder. "Colin? It's midnight."

"Already?" He blinked and stared down at his watch. Scrubbing his hands over his face, he swung upright. "Thanks, Aiden. I take it you didn't see anything unusual?"

"Not really. I was worried for a while, though."

"Why?" His sleepiness vanished. "What happened?"

"Nothing really happened. I noticed a boat out on the lake moving slowly past the house. I know it's a no wake zone after dark, but it drew my attention. I watched as it continued cruising all the way down to the other side of the lake, then turned around to make its way back along the opposite shore. I grabbed my binocs from my duffel and examined it more closely. Four people on board, two men and two women. Decided it was tourists taking in the sights."

"Yeah, that makes sense." He relaxed. "Do you mind if I use the binocs? Might be helpful if more boats head out on the water."

"Of course." Aiden grinned. "They are not everyday binocs either. They have night vision lenses too."

He couldn't help smiling back. "Soldiers like to be prepared, huh?"

"Something like that." Aiden shrugged. "I figured I'd bring as much of my gear as possible."

"Good decision, thanks." He stood and accepted the small pair of binoculars Aiden held out for him. He took a moment to familiarize himself with how they worked, using the night vision lenses to scan the darkness outside the window. "Wow, these are great."

"Yep." Aiden yawned. "Get out, bro. It's my turn to get some sleep."

"You bet." He had stretched out fully clothed in case they needed to make a quick getaway. He quickly put his shoes on, then headed for the door. "I'll let you know if I find anything."

"Sounds good. But I don't think you will. It's a nice, quiet community out here." Aiden grinned then closed the bedroom door behind him.

Colin softly crept down the stairs to the main level. He took a moment to peer through the front and back windows, before ducking in to use the bathroom. In the kitchen, he poured himself a large glass of water, wondering if he should make coffee. He hesitated, not wanting to disturb Faye.

He quietly eased down the hall to the master suite. He listened for several long moments but heard nothing from inside. Reassured she was asleep, he returned to the kitchen to brew the pot of coffee.

Between the caffeine and the four hours of sleep, he was struck by a renewed energy. He silently agreed with his brother that the rest of the night would be quiet, but of course, that didn't mean he would let his guard down.

Fascinated by the night vision lenses and the odd green hue that enabled him to see clearly, he went from one window to the next, examining the area around the house. While looking at the wooded area to the right, stopping when he saw a large deer moving through the trees. No rack, so he assumed she was a doe. Then he noticed the smaller deer beside her. Doe and her fawn, he guessed.

A wide smile creased his features. Amazing.

Satisfied there was no threat lurking nearby, he sat at the kitchen table in the dark, sipping his coffee. Staying up and alert gave him a new appreciation for the work his cop siblings did. He could sleep or eat during his downtime at the fire station. Not that they didn't get plenty of paramedic calls, because they did.

That made him think of his youngest sister, Elly. She'd been working as an EMT for a few months now, and so far she seemed to enjoy it. She talked a lot about the transfers they did between nursing homes and the hospital for patients who needed care. He and the rest of the family had been concerned when Elly hadn't been able to settle on a career.

Not that she hadn't tried. Elly first wanted to be a cop but hadn't been able to pass the physical requirements, and then she had ended up quitting nursing school after two years in the program. She'd met with a military recruiter, but then she had decided the same physical requirements required for the academy would hold her back.

Rhy had encouraged her to consider other professions— accounting, marketing, whatever might interest her. But Elly had been determined to carry on the family tradition of being a first responder.

When she'd started the EMT program, they'd secretly wondered how long this career choice would last. Aiden had wanted to run a pool guessing the length of time she'd stick with it, but Rhy had shut that down. Their oldest brother had made a point of reminding them they were all going to support Elly.

No matter what.

So they had. And she'd been doing well. Although he also had sensed a faint trepidation in Elly's eyes on the few occasions he'd been there when she'd headed off to work.

Nerves probably. One thing about being a paramedic or an EMT, you never knew what you would find when the next call came in. He'd seen some tragic cases up close and personal. And it worried him a bit that Elly's soft heart would take a beating in this job.

Finishing his first cup of coffee, he poured another, then made rounds again. As he watched through the patio doors overlooking the lake, he frowned when he noticed a small rowboat.

Picking up the binocs, he looked at the occupant for a long time. The person rowing the boat across the lake was a male, who appeared relatively young, maybe in his late teens. He didn't seem to look at the houses along the shore, though, but simply rowed the boat over the calm surface of the water.

Rather unusual to be out rowing a boat in the middle of the night. But as he looked again through the binocs and night vision lenses, he didn't see a weapon. There was no sign of an accelerant either. No boat engine meant there wasn't any gasoline. The kid simply took long deep strokes, gliding across the water. Training maybe for a college rowing team.

Colin let out a long sigh, reminding himself not to over-react. A teenager rowing a boat after midnight was hardly a threat.

Strange, maybe. But not something to be concerned about.

After his third set of rounds, Colin dropped down onto the sofa for a few minutes. He wasn't tired, but the boredom was killing him.

The sound of a door opening had him shooting to his feet. He moved toward the master suite as Faye came out of the room.

"What's wrong? Are you okay?" He raked his gaze over her, wondering if something had frightened her.

"I smelled coffee and thought it might be morning." She grimaced. "I didn't realize it was one thirty until I was up and out of bed."

A stab of guilt hit hard. "I didn't mean to wake you."

She waved a hand. "You didn't. My sleep schedule is all messed up from working so many night shifts in a row."

"Go back to bed, Faye. There's still plenty of time to rest before morning."

She shook her head and dropped down at the table. "I tried. My brain started going through each of the attacks against me. It's depressing to realize someone hates me enough to do this."

"Hey, they don't necessarily hate you personally." He

sat beside her, even though his instincts were warning him not to get too close. He was supposed to be on guard duty, not thinking about kissing her. "If Jayson Sanders is the one behind this, he's mad at your father. Maybe even at women in general since his sexual harassment is what got him fired in the first place."

"I hadn't thought about it from that perspective, but you could be right. I might be the person he targeted because he knows he can't go after all the female firefighters he harassed."

"Exactly." He lightly patted her arm, then abruptly stood. "I need to make rounds. You should really try to get some sleep."

"Rounds?" She looked at the binocs in his hand. "Oh, you've been spying out the windows."

"Not spying." She made him sound like a kid playing a game. "Being on alert for danger. I already saw a young kid rowing his boat down the lake."

"At this hour?" Her eyebrows levered upward. "That's odd."

"Yes, which is why I need to continually make rounds." He didn't add that the more distance he kept between the two of them, the better. He moved to the front window. It took a moment for him to get the binocs and the night vision lenses focused.

He moved the glasses slowly so that he wouldn't miss anything. Then he abruptly stopped. Was that a car?

He zoomed in to get a better look. Yes, there was a car sitting several yards down the road. He lowered the glasses with a frown. There had not been a car there fifteen to twenty minutes ago.

The kid in the rowboat?

An abrupt flash of light blinded him. He dropped the

night vision lenses, blinking to clear his vision. The lenses were only good in the darkness, and for a moment, he wondered if the driver of the car had known that he was using them.

Impossible, but the paranoia remained.

"Look out!" Faye shouted.

He instinctively jumped backward as the sound of breaking glass echoed around him. The acrid scent of accelerant hit hard.

When his vision cleared, he saw the fire.

CHAPTER THIRTEEN

"Colin!" Seeing fire, she lunged forward, desperate to reach Colin.

"Stay back!" Colin's sharp tone stopped her cold. Hearing more breaking glass, she understood what was happening.

They were under attack!

She shrank back from the fire that was quickly spreading wherever the accelerant had spilled. Aiden's footsteps pounded as he came down to see what was going on.

A third window shattered. Glancing down the short hall to the master suite, she realized the bed was on fire.

The lake house would be destroyed if the arsonist kept this up.

A fourth window shattered. Soon the entire house would be engulfed in flames!

"Colin, we need to get down to the lakefront." Aiden's calm tone helped calm her nerves. "There are too many points of entry. You can't put the fire out by yourself."

"I know." He abruptly turned from where he was attempting to smother the flames licking the floor and chair with a throw blanket. Darting between the steadily growing flames, he quickly joined them. He held his left arm awkwardly against his body. It took a moment for her to realize his arm had been injured.

"You're burned!" Faye stared in horror. All the hair on his arm was gone, singed from the fire. She quickly turned and grabbed a towel from the kitchen drawer. She took precious seconds to thoroughly douse the hand towel in icy cold water. Then she came over to gingerly wrap it around his reddened arm. "This will help draw out the heat to slow the burn process. But we need to get you to the hospital ASAP."

"I'll be fine." His gaze was somber as he glanced back at the fire. "We need the keys to the boat."

"Keys." She stared at him blankly. The fire was spreading, smoke rising and making her cough. It was almost like being in the restrooms at the park. "I don't know where they are."

"I have them." Aiden held up the boat key dangling from a small bright-yellow flotation device. "Noticed where they were kept earlier."

"Great. Let's go." Colin put his uninjured arm around her as Aiden led the way through the patio doors. The fresh air was a blessing, and she took several deep breaths to clear her lungs. She couldn't understand how any smoker willingly filled their lungs with smoke. Her throat felt as if it were on fire from being abused these past few days.

Aiden didn't hesitate to lead the way down to the lakeshore. The rental boat was still up in the lift, but Aiden seemed to know what to do. He deftly lowered the boat into the water, then jumped inside to man the wheel.

"Hurry," Colin urged, holding out his hand so she could

step up. "We need to be out of here before the arsonist investigates our escape route."

Imagining what would happen if another firebomb was tossed into the boat had her quickly climbing inside. She'd only been on this boat once two years ago, but she trusted both of these Finnegans with her life. With only one good hand, Colin released the ties and pushed the boat backward, out of the lift.

Aiden started the engine and shifted into reverse. Moments later, Colin dropped into the seat across from her, distributing their weight evenly as Aiden turned the wheel so they could head out across the water. Despite the no wake after dusk rule, Aiden pushed the throttle forward, picking up speed to put as much distance between them and the lake house as possible.

She looked back over her shoulder at the fire that was raging inside the rental property. Numbly she realized this had been a bad decision. Not only had they been found, but this house would likely be destroyed much as her personal home had been.

A dark figure ran down toward the lake. The arsonist! She grabbed Colin's arm. "There he is!"

Colin turned to see the figure in black standing near the boat lift. As if sensing their gaze, the arsonist quickly turned and ran back up to the side of the house.

"Aiden, we need to go back." Colin gestured with his uninjured arm. "He's getting away."

"We're not going back," Aiden said flatly. "We're armed, but we have no idea what sort of firepower he has at his fingertips. We're not taking that risk."

"I guess you're right." Colin sounded dejected. "Just before the first firebomb crashed through the window, I noticed a sedan parked several yards down the road. I'm sure the arsonist is gone by now."

"If he was smart, he would be," Aiden agreed. "Do you have your phone? Call 911 to report the fire and the arsonist."

"Will do." Colin quickly made the call, urging caution to those responding to the fire in case the arsonist was still hanging around nearby. When he finished, he sighed heavily. "I hope we're not putting anyone else in danger."

"Not us, the arsonist," Aiden corrected.

Colin grimaced but didn't say anything more.

"I want to know how we're going to catch this guy." She glanced between the two Finnegans as they raced to the other side of the lake. "He seems to constantly be one step ahead of us. And I really don't understand how he found us here."

"I've been thinking about that too." Colin shook his head. "The only answer I can come up with is that your father must have talked about this rental property to other members within the firefighting family. I never heard anything about it, but someone must have known to search for you here."

She found that horrifying. "I don't know why my dad would talk about it."

"Me either," Aiden agreed. "But he may not have bothered to keep it a secret."

She thought it more likely Claire had bragged about it, but that didn't explain how the arsonist had known.

"We'll have to think through how we set the trap at the American Lodge," Colin said slowly. "Using the phone to draw him out is good, but how will we prevent him from just tossing more firebombs through the window like he did here?"

"That's a good point." Aiden shrugged. "I think we'll need to keep the room empty and have more firefighting backup readily available."

"Maybe we shouldn't risk burning down the motel," she felt compelled to point out. "It's Gary's livelihood."

"You're right about that. We'll have to think of something else." Colin's voice was subdued. "Maybe we can find a place that we can set up as fireproof ahead of time. Or at least minimize the potential fire damage."

There was a long silence as they digested that thought. Finally, Aiden spoke. "If we hadn't taken turns being on watch for trouble, I don't think we'd have been able to escape so quickly. Not without being seriously injured."

"You're right, Aiden. God was with us tonight." Her gaze landed on Colin's arm. He'd been hurt, but she understood the outcome could have been so much worse.

Aiden pulled back on the throttle as he reached the public boat launch. He pulled over to the side of a pier, and Colin threw a line around one of the posts, drawing them in.

"We'll have to call Rhy," Aiden said as they climbed out of the vessel. "We can't risk going back to the lake house for our vehicles. We have to assume the arsonist has damaged my truck in some way. And your SUV is in the garage, too, close to the fire for comfort."

"Yes, I noticed there were several gas cans in the garage, probably for the boat. We don't want to be anywhere nearby if the fire reaches the garage." Colin shook his head. "But it will take at least two hours for Rhy to get here."

"I know." Aiden gestured toward the path leading to the road. "Let's go."

She and Colin followed his lead. But even as they walked along the side of the road, listening as Aiden made the call to Rhy, she fought an overwhelming wave of despair.

How many more fires would the arsonist start in his thirst for revenge?

How much longer before this nightmare came to an end?

———

HIS ARM HURT, but Colin did his best to ignore it, knowing it could have been much worse. He hated knowing he'd made so many mistakes in his quest to keep Faye safe.

And this was why he wasn't a cop. He tried to approach this the way his older brothers would, but he'd failed miserably.

Based on this most recent incident, he knew staying at the homestead and dropping Faye at her father's house were both out of the question. They were walking magnets for this arsonist. If he didn't know better, he'd think this guy had superpowers.

"Okay, Rhy, Devon, Tarin, and Joy are all on the way, they're bringing two cars," Aiden said.

"Why so many?" Faye asked.

Aiden shrugged. "The guys don't want to leave their wives home alone. I can't say that I blame them."

"Yeah, especially Devon as she's pregnant." Colin felt awful for waking them up in the middle of the night. "I wish we didn't have to put them out like this."

"They assured me they'd rather be here to help," Aiden said. He met his glance. "Speaking of which, I think you should call Mitch Callahan too."

"I was planning to wait until morning." He waved a

hand at the homes within the Fish Lake community. "It's not as if this is his jurisdiction."

"I get it, but he may want to examine the scene regardless," Aiden said.

He dug out his phone, then looked at Faye. "I don't suppose you have your new phone with you."

"I do." She lifted the phone. "It's still off, though. I double-checked to make sure we weren't tracked that way."

"Good." That was one less problem to worry about. Not that there weren't plenty of other hurdles to overcome. With one hand, he thumbed the screen to reach his recent calls. Mitch was near the top. He squashed a flash of guilt for waking him up, knowing his second cousin had two small kids at home.

There were several rings before he heard Mitch's groggy voice. "What's wrong?"

"I'm sorry to wake you, but there's been another attempt against Faye. Unfortunately, we're well out of your jurisdiction; we're in Wautoma at Fish Lake."

"Fish Lake?" Mitch's tone sounded more alert now. "Oh yeah, the rental property. What happened?"

He quickly filled Mitch in on the details. "This time the arsonist came prepared with multiple firebombs, either Molotov cocktails or something similar. Each one was tossed through a window. The fire spread rapidly after that. We escaped by boat and are currently still sitting out here waiting for Rhy and Tarin to arrive."

"I don't like it," Mitch muttered. "How did this guy find you?"

"I wish I knew. We thought it would be safe since the property wasn't in Dorian's name. But maybe the rental property was easier to find than we realized."

"Maybe. Anything is possible," Mitch agreed.

"Colin?" Faye placed her hand on his uninjured arm. "I've been thinking about that. It could be that Claire has been blabbing about the lake house. She's active on social media; she may have posted pictures there too. It may not have been as much of a secret as we thought."

"I heard that," Mitch said. "Faye could be right. If someone had taken the time to research the chief's life before lashing out in revenge, they may have followed his wife on social media and found out about the lake house."

"Yeah, well, we need to reconsider our plan to use the American Lodge." Colin swept his gaze over the area but didn't see anything concerning. "We can't risk Gary losing his business to this guy."

"What we need is a place with bulletproof windows, something to prevent forced entry," Mitch said with a sigh. "I'll think about that more, but in the meantime, what do you need from me?"

"First, you should know the vehicle you loaned me is in the garage of the lake house." He winced, anticipating Mitch's anger. "I'm sorry, but I have no idea if it will burn with the rest of the property or not."

"That's okay. Things can be replaced. People cannot." Mitch didn't sound nearly as upset as he'd expected. "We'll take care of that later. I'm just glad you three escaped without being hurt."

"Me too." He didn't mention his arm. "Thanks for being so understanding."

"Do you have the address?" Mitch asked. "I'll have to head up there and talk to the locals."

The sound of sirens filled the air, making it difficult to hear Mitch on the other end of the call. The fire response had been quicker than he'd anticipated considering the lake property was in a small town. "I'll text you," he shouted into the line.

Unable to hear Mitch's response, he lowered the phone. With one hand, he ended the call, then scrolled to find the address. He didn't like being hampered this way and hoped the burn on his forearm wasn't too serious.

Protecting Faye would be difficult if he couldn't use both hands.

As if reading his mind, she plucked the phone from his hands and typed in the address for the lake property. Then handed it back. She moved closer to speak into his ear. "Let's go meet up with the ambulance. I need to take a closer look at your arm."

He nodded, reluctantly understanding it was the smart thing to do. Once she could treat his arm properly, he may be able to use it.

The three of them continued walking down the road toward the lake house. The yellow fire was like a beacon in the night. Aiden went first, carrying his weapon and holding it ready. He kept Faye between them so that he could cover her back. He held Mitch's backup weapon in his hand too.

Taking precautions was smart, but he didn't think the arsonist had lingered. Not after verifying they'd escaped via boat.

No, he felt certain the guy was long gone and already planning his next move.

Fifteen minutes later, they reached the fire response posted outside the burning lake house. He stared at the fire for a long moment, dejected at the way the entire lower level of the building was engulfed in flames.

"There's the ambulance." Faye tugged him toward it.

Aiden came with them, still alert for any possible

threats. When they reached the ambulance, Faye approached the two EMTs standing outside, watching the crew work to bring the fire under control.

"I'm Dr. Faye Kimble. I work in the ED at Trinity Medical Center." She gestured toward their kit. "I have an injured firefighter here. May I please use your supplies?"

"He's not dressed like a firefighter," the shorter man said.

"We were inside the building when the fire started." There was a hint of impatience in Faye's tone. "I really need to dress his wound."

"Here, take what you need." The taller of the two men reached over to open the medical kit. "I have a brother who works in Milwaukee. He told me how impressed he was with the care provided at Trinity."

Faye's features softened. "Thank you. We can pay you for the supplies."

"No need." The taller guy waved that off. "It's fine."

Colin touched the wet towel Faye had wrapped around his arm. It was warm to the touch, which surprised him.

"I'm going to use cold packs first," Faye explained. "See if we can pull more heat out from your skin."

The cold packs eased some of the pain, although his skin felt raw and tender. Yet he'd expected his arm to look much worse than it did, so he swallowed the discomfort.

"We're going to use the cold packs until your brother picks us up." Faye wrapped gauze around his arm, holding the cold packs in place. "Then I'll apply the burn cream."

"Sounds good." He'd taken care of minor burn injuries as a paramedic, but it was strange to be on the receiving end of care. He was grateful for Faye's expertise.

"I wish I could check out the truck." Aiden frowned at

the firefighters swarming the property, using hoses to put out the fire. "From here it looks fine."

"They're not going to let you get close." Colin empathized with his younger brother. Aiden and Elly still lived at the homestead, as Aiden had been saving up for a house. Now it looked like he'd need to sink some money into a replacement vehicle. "I'm sorry."

"Nah, it's fine." Aiden sighed. "I guess I don't like the idea of sitting around here waiting for our brothers to arrive."

"We could take you to the closest hospital," the taller EMT offered. "From there you could grab a rideshare."

"Hey, we're not supposed to do that," the short guy protested. "You trying to get us fired?"

"That's a sweet offer," Faye said with a smile. "But I don't want either of you to risk your jobs. We'll wait here."

Lingering at the scene when he wasn't involved in fighting the fire wasn't easy. Colin hated feeling helpless. The minutes crept by with agonizing slowness as the fire crew continued dousing the fire.

When they'd finished, the fire captain came over to talk to them. "Which one of you was inside when this happened?"

"All three of us were inside." Colin stepped forward. "I'm a firefighter from Milwaukee, and I want to thank you for your quick response."

"You get burned?" The captain gestured to his arm.

"Yeah. I was standing near the window when it shattered." Colin went on to explain what had transpired and how they'd escaped.

"And you don't have any idea who is behind this?" The captain eyed him suspiciously.

"I promise that if I did, I would tell you and every other

cop within the state." He tried not to sound as bitterly frustrated as he felt. "We've been dodging this arsonist for the past two days. I have yet to get a clear view of his face."

"You mentioned seeing the sedan," Aiden reminded him. "Anything about the vehicle stand out in your mind?"

He took a moment to think back to those moments before he realized the arsonist had found them. "It was a dark vehicle with four doors. There may have been a bumper sticker on the right side of the rear bumper, but I can't say that for sure. My view was mostly of the passenger-side rear quarter panel."

The captain frowned. "Where was it?"

Colin walked over to the area where he'd seen the sedan. Surprisingly, the fire trucks weren't in the way, having come up to the front of the house. He frowned when he noticed a dark spot on the road. Dabbing it with his finger, he noticed a dampness there. "Here. Looks like the sedan might be leaking oil. This is fresh."

Aiden hunkered down at the side of the road to see it more closely. He tapped the spot with his index finger and lifted it to his nose. "Yeah, it's oil."

"Not much of a clue," the captain said grimly.

Colin silently agreed. He wished he'd gotten a clearer view of the arsonist's face. At the time, he'd thought the guy looked a bit like the kid in the rowboat.

Now he wasn't sure about anything. Especially his ability to keep his promise to Chief Kimble.

"Colin? I see a car approaching." Faye's voice interrupted his thoughts.

"Good." He turned from the site, taking Faye's hand. "It's well past time for us to get out of here."

Aiden quickened his pace to join them. Colin abruptly stopped when he only saw one vehicle. When it stopped, and Rhy stepped out, he realized Tarin would be coming from farther south where his home was located.

"You neglected to tell me that you were injured." Rhy scowled at the large bandage covering his arm. "What happened?"

"A minor burn. It's nothing." He managed a weak smile. "Thanks for coming."

Rhy turned toward Faye. "Is he really okay?"

"He will be. Thankfully, it's not as bad as I feared." She gestured to the items on the ground at her feet. "I have a fresh box of gauze and burn cream to use on the way back to Milwaukee."

Rhy shook his head, then glanced to where the firefighters were putting their gear away. "This guy is serious, Colin."

"I know." A second pair of headlights cut through the darkness. Tarin and Joy had arrived. "We're not going back to the homestead with you. I'm hoping you'll let us borrow your vehicle."

Rhy hesitated, glancing at Tarin who came over to join them. "I don't mind handing over my vehicle, but we need to do something more. Find a way to get this guy before he strikes again."

"Yeah, I couldn't agree more." Tarin glanced at his injury but didn't comment. "What's the plan?"

Colin had no idea. "I'm open to suggestions. So far, every single one of my ideas has been an abject failure."

"Don't say that," Faye protested. "This isn't your fault. We're alive because of you and Aiden."

He didn't look at her, his gaze trained on his brother. "I'm not a cop, Rhy. I'm not sure what we should do."

"I know of a safe house you can use for the rest of the weekend," Tarin said. "I'll call to make the arrangements."

"Is that going to cause trouble for you with the upper brass?" Colin knew his brother was likely taking a risk. Milwaukee PD safe houses weren't for general use.

"I'll be okay. This is a relatively new place that was set up for a particular case. It's perfect for this." Tarin waved aside his concern. "It's obvious you and Faye need to be safe."

"How about we all head to the safe house together? Tarin and Joy can drop us off at the homestead afterward. I have the weekend off, so we don't need to use the car."

Colin was humbled by how readily his family rallied around them. "Thanks, Rhy, and you too, Tarin."

"Let's hit the road, then." Aiden looked impatient. "The truck is saturated, much of the paint bubbled from the heat. The tires were slashed too. I'll have to get it towed to the closest garage once this is over."

"I'll pay for the damage," Colin offered.

"It's okay. I'll take care of it." Aiden grinned. "Rhy and Devon will just have to put up with me for a while longer."

"That's not a problem," Devon spoke up. "You can help with the baby."

Despite the seriousness of the situation, the look of horror that crossed Aiden's features made Colin laugh. Aiden and a baby, that was a good one.

They split up, Aiden driving Tarin's car, with Tarin and Joy in the back so Tare could make the safe house arrangements. He and Faye hitched a ride with Rhy and Devon.

It was a long drive back to the city, but when they finally reached the safe house, Colin had to admit being impressed. The nondescript brick house had a security system, and the windows were made of bullet-resistant glass.

He exchanged a glance with Aiden who nodded in

silent agreement. They were both thinking the same thing. This was the perfect place to use as a trap for the arsonist. He silently prayed that doing so wouldn't put Tarin's job on the line.

His family had done so much for him. He didn't want to cause any more trouble for them than he had already.

Yet if they didn't grab this guy and soon, he feared they wouldn't escape the next attempt.

CHAPTER FOURTEEN

The safe house looked innocuous from the outside, but Faye was glad to find the interior neat and clean. Bare, without much decoration, but that wasn't a problem. The air was a bit stale from the place being closed up, but that was the least of her worries. She was impressed by the security system and the bullet-resistant glass.

This was probably the safest place they'd been in the past forty-eight hours. She couldn't simply stay here forever, but the secure feeling was nice.

"I want to look at your arm again." She gestured for Colin to take a seat.

He did so, and she unwrapped the arm she'd covered in the car on the drive back to the city. The burn cream she'd liberally applied coated his arm. Looking at it more closely, she could see there was only one small area that appeared to be a second-degree burn. The rest of the skin was still red, but she deemed that area to be only a first-degree burn. "Looks fairly good, but we'll need to change the dressings at least twice a day."

"Thanks, doc."

She glanced up at him. "How is your pain?"

"I'm fine." He shrugged off her concern. "I'm just glad it's not worse."

"Me too." She hated knowing he'd been hurt at all. "I'll take another look at it tomorrow. We may need more supplies, though. I could only take so much from the EMTs on scene."

"We'll work on that later." He didn't appear concerned. "Thanks, Faye."

Her body craved sleep. Her mind, however, whirled like a tornado. Her adrenaline had been up and down so often she could understand why it was difficult to relax.

"I like this place," Aiden said. "It's a nice option."

"Agreed." Colin glanced around. "I just hope Tarin doesn't get in trouble for allowing us to use it."

"He won't." Aiden sounded confident, while it was obvious Colin didn't agree.

"It's going on five-thirty in the morning, we should try to get some rest." Colin rose from his seat at the table. "We'll discuss a game plan later."

From the way the brothers exchanged a glance, she felt certain they already had a plan in mind. They wouldn't do anything now, though, so she made her way down the hall to the master bedroom. The Finnegan brothers had insisted she use that one for the privacy of having her own bathroom.

They were the kindest and most considerate guys she'd ever met. Tears pricked her eyes, but she quickly wiped them away. She wasn't one to break down crying, yet the culmination of stress, anxiety, and fear over the past few days was obviously catching up with her.

She stood at the window for a long moment, gazing up at the sky. Despite the early hour, dawn was brightening the horizon to the east. Closing her eyes, she silently prayed for God to continue watching over them and for His guidance in bringing the arsonist to justice.

Before any innocent people were hurt.

Faye wasn't sure how she'd managed to fall asleep, but when she awoke, bright sunlight streamed in through the window. Peering at the clock, she noticed it was almost nine o'clock in the morning.

After a quick shower, she headed to the kitchen, following the scent of freshly brewed coffee. No surprise to find Colin already up.

"Did you get any sleep?" She was concerned about him. There were dark circles beneath his eyes.

"I did." He flashed a wry smile and shrugged. "Only about two hours, though. My body clock is a mess. My brain kept telling me it was time to be up."

"I know that feeling." She poured a cup of coffee, then joined him at the table. "I didn't ask last night, but what sort of food is stocked here?"

"Aiden called in an order for groceries and more gauze too." Colin glanced at his watch. "Should be delivered here soon. Then I'll make breakfast."

"You're always offering to cook." She smiled as she sipped her coffee. "I can handle easy stuff like eggs and toast."

He chuckled. "I don't mind. And I ordered bacon too. No breakfast is complete without bacon."

That made her laugh. "Sounds good."

They were silent for a moment, enjoying the morning light and delicious coffee. Finally, she decided to ask, "When are you going to fill me in on the plan you and Aiden have already come up with?"

He shook his head, a wry grin tugging at his mouth. "You're too smart for your own good."

"Yeah, I've been told that before." She didn't take offense. "That's what got me through medical school. Come on, Colin. Fill me in. I assume we're not heading to the American Lodge."

"That's correct." His expression turned grim. "I don't want to risk Gary losing his motel in a fire."

"I agree, I don't want that to happen either." Then it dawned on her. "You're going to use this place." She waved a hand at the room. "Because the windows are bullet resistant."

"Like I said, too smart for your own good." He nodded. "We are considering that, yes. But we need to find a safe place for you to wait. After the lake house fiasco, I don't want you anywhere near the arsonist."

"I want to be where you are." Her cheeks grew warm as she realized he could read into that statement. "I feel safe with you. I don't want us to be separated."

"I'm humbled by your trust, especially since I've done nothing but put you in danger." His low voice held a hint of anguish. "I should have done better."

"You did everything right." It wasn't his fault the arsonist had managed to figure out their locations. She reached over to take his uninjured hand in hers. "I am so thankful you've been here with me through all of this."

Their gazes met and held, a shimmer of attraction enveloping them like a cloak. She wished he'd kiss her again. A sharp knock at the door had them breaking apart.

"I've got it." Aiden came out of his room, a towel slung over his shoulders, his reddish hair damp. He took a moment to peer through the peephole to verify the delivery man's identity before opening the door. "Thanks." Aiden passed the young woman a folded bill, then picked up the box. Holding it under one arm, he closed and locked the door.

"Time to make breakfast." Colin stood and unpacked the box, setting items on the counter that he planned to use right away.

Faye jumped up to help as Aiden went back to his room to finish washing up. Colin used both his hands to begin preparing breakfast. Since the worst of the burn was midway up his forearm, she didn't protest.

His burn injury could have been so much worse.

"Sit down," he said, glancing at her. "I don't need you hovering."

"Okay." She refilled her cup and sat. "I still don't understand how you and Aiden intend to use the safe house to draw the arsonist out of hiding. I mean, I get how you'll use my phone, hoping to lure him here. But he's been attacking from afar. How do we make sure he doesn't get away this time?"

Colin nodded as he cooked bacon in one pan, using the other for the eggs. "Aiden and I discussed that issue too. We'll talk to Rhy about having some of the guys from his tactical team stationed nearby as backup."

She envisioned several guys hidden around the property, waiting for the arsonist to show up. It was a good idea except for the part where the arsonist would have accelerants or other flammable material with him. "Maybe you need a fire truck nearby too."

"I thought of that, but a rig would be too noticeable." He shrugged, glancing at her over his shoulder. "I figure notifying the fire station the minute this guy shows is our best option."

"That may not be fast enough to prevent anyone from

being burned." The more she heard about this so-called plan, the less she liked it. "There has to be another way."

"We'll discuss it more with Rhy. If he has other options, we're open to hearing them." Colin flipped the eggs, then turned to face her. "But we need to stop this guy today. Once and for all."

"I know." She wanted that too. More than anything. Letting the issue drop, she rose. "Do you want me to make toast?"

"Sure."

They sat down to eat five minutes later. As before, Colin led the before-meal prayer. "Lord Jesus, we thank You for this food and for keeping us safe in Your loving care. We ask for Your continued wisdom and guidance as we strive to prevent this man from hurting anyone else. In Jesus's name. Amen."

"Amen." She lifted her head to look at Colin. "That was nice."

"We'll need all of God's support to get through this." He picked up his fork and scooped up some eggs. "And we can't do anything on an empty stomach."

"Truth, brother." Aiden took a bite of bacon. "Thanks for cooking breakfast."

"Any time."

Faye savored the meal, instinctively dreading what the rest of the day may bring. When they were finished, she stacked the dishes on the counter and offered to clean up. "It's the least I can do."

"Thanks, Faye." Colin filled his cup with coffee and turned to Aiden. "How much longer should we wait to contact Rhy?"

"It's almost ten." Aiden shrugged. "Rhy and Devon usually attend church services at this time."

"I forgot it's Sunday." Colin groaned. "Normally, we'd join them if we weren't working."

"I'm sure we'll be forgiven for skipping out." Aiden set his empty cup on the sink. She dropped it into the sudsy water. "I need walk around outside, check the layout of the area more closely. You should stay here with Faye."

"Okay." She was a little surprised Colin didn't argue. "You're the soldier, Aiden. I'm just a firefighter."

"A very good one too. Lock up after me." Aiden moved toward the door. Colin did so, then returned to the kitchen.

"You still attend church with your family?" Having been exposed to their deep faith, she shouldn't have been surprised.

"When we're not working." He grinned. "The family church is in Brookland, not exactly close to where I live, but we generally have Sunday dinner together, so we make it an all-day affair. Of course, that's much more fun in the fall when we can watch football too."

She had no interest in sports but sensed the Finnegan gatherings were more about spending family time together than the games themselves. An entire day of togetherness was something she hadn't experienced since her mother had died. "Sounds really nice."

"You're welcome to join us anytime," he offered. "We'd love to have you."

"Maybe when this is over." She was secretly thrilled by his offer but tried not to read too much into it. Colin was being his usual nice and friendly self. She had no doubt Aiden would have made the same offer, even though there was absolutely no chemistry between them.

No, the constant sense of awareness she felt was just with Colin. She turned her attention to finishing the dishes.

If Colin and Aiden could make this plan of theirs work, today could very well be their last time together.

By tomorrow morning, they'd go their separate ways.

COLIN TORE his gaze from Faye, forcing himself to concentrate on the mission ahead. He'd have to look around outside, too, when Aiden was finished. They all needed to be familiar with the barriers that may crop up as they executed this plan.

And that all depended on Rhy and his guys lending a hand. Two men, one who wasn't a cop, couldn't keep a close enough eye on the place. He was especially concerned with the houses on either side of them. They didn't seem too close, but he knew how easily the dancing dragon could spin out of control. Tarin would be in enough trouble by loaning them the safe house. If they caused damage to the homes around them, his brother could lose his job.

He'd racked his brain last night, trying to come up with another place that might work. He'd considered using his personal condo, but the shared wall with another residence and the lack of bullet-resistant glass made that a less optimal option.

It troubled him to put Tarin's job on the line, so he decided to call his brother Brady. In his role within the FBI, there may be another safe house option. When the call went to voice mail, he belatedly realized Brady, Grace, and their son, Caleb, may be in church too.

What they needed was a family meeting. He shot his brother Rhy a text, knowing his phone would be off in church but that he'd check his messages as soon as the service was finished.

Family meeting at SH. Call when able.

To his surprise, his brother texted back. *Good idea. Will call soon.*

Aiden knocked at the door. Colin peered through the peephole, then unlocked the door to let Aiden inside. As he shot the dead bolts home, two of them, he asked, "What did you think?"

"It'll work. It's not perfect, but the closest houses are far enough away that the occupants shouldn't be in danger."

"Rhy and the others will be here soon. I called a family meeting." He raked his hand over his hair. "Brady may have another option for us too."

"Good idea. But we can't wait too long." Aiden's gaze was serious. "This guy hasn't slowed down since this mess started. We need to set the trap ASAP."

"I know." He felt the same sense of urgency. If they didn't go on offense, they'd be forced back into defensive mode.

By noon, a large part of the family was gathered in the safe house. Quinn and Sami, along with Alanna and Elly were missing, each on duty in their respective jobs today. The Finnegans had left their respective spouses at home too.

"I like the idea of using Faye's phone as a lure," Rhy said. "Not sure we should use this place for that, though."

"I know," Colin admitted, glancing at Tarin. "We don't want to cause you trouble."

"Believe it or not, I was able to finagle approval from my boss." Tarin shrugged. "I promised to pay for any repairs or damage, so if we could keep that to a minimum, it would be great."

"We can help with that," Kyleigh spoke up. She was a

sheriff's deputy and recently married ADA Bax Scala. "Money isn't as important as keeping Faye safe."

"We'll handle the financial side of things," Rhy said firmly. Colin knew his oldest sibling didn't like taking advantage of Kyleigh's wealthy husband. Bax earned a modest salary in his job working for the state of Wisconsin as an ADA, but he had also inherited money from his grandparents' estate. Savvy investing had doubled the amount over the years. "And if that's the only barrier, then we should execute our plan here."

"I agree," Brady said. "We could find another safe house, but I can't guarantee bullet-resistant windows." He looked around in admiration. "Looks like the feds need to up their game. This place is great."

"Keep in mind that bullet-resistant windows won't prevent the arsonist from starting a fire outside," Colin warned. "He could easily douse the exterior with gasoline or some other accelerant and light it up. The exterior is mostly brick, but there's wood window frames and some siding."

"I hear you," Rhy said. "And that's kind of the point of this idea, isn't it? To draw this guy out into the open, forcing his hand so we can arrest him."

"Shouldn't Mitch Callahan be involved?" Faye asked. She'd been unusually quiet during the discussion, maybe daunted by the number of Finnegans in the room.

"Normally, yes." He glanced at his brothers and Kyleigh. "He has a family, and I was thinking it would be better if we leave him out of this part. You too, Rhy. With Devon expecting, it would be best if you would let the rest of us handle this."

"Yeah, that's not happening. And Callahan won't like being excluded either," Rhy pointed out. "But I understand your perspective. As the arson investigator, he's the one we call once we have a suspected arson event, so we can hold off for now. I've called Joe Kingsley and a few of my tactical guys. They're ready and willing to help. I'm confident in my team's ability to protect us."

"I take it they're volunteering for this mission?" Colin asked.

"They are." Rhy grinned. "We're calling it a training session."

"What time do we bait the trap?" Brady asked.

"I was originally thinking we should wait until later tonight." Colin grimaced. "But it would be easier for all of us if we set the trap earlier than later."

"I agree," Aiden said. "This guy has struck during the daytime before. No reason to think he wouldn't do so again now."

"Staying well hidden during the daytime won't be easy." Kyleigh frowned. "And even if we set the trap later this afternoon, there's no guarantee what time this guy will show up."

"That would be true no matter what time we set the trap." Colin glanced at each of his siblings. "You guys are the experts, what do you think?"

"We set the trap at four p.m.," Rhy said. "That gives us time to get my guys into position. Colin, we need you and Faye to be settled nearby too. Preferably with one of us guarding you."

"I'm armed and can take care of myself." Colin glanced at Faye, who nodded.

"I can watch Colin's back," Aiden offered.

"Works for me." Rhy rose to his feet. "I'm going to notify my guys. They'll need time to get geared up and settled in place."

They hammered out the rest of the details over the next hour. By three thirty, they were ready to go. Faye took out her phone, powered it up, and used it to call her father.

"Hey, Dad, just want you to know I'm still doing well." Her gaze clung to Colin's as she spoke. He shook his head, indicating she shouldn't go into detail about the fire at the lake house rental yet. They needed to set the phone down in the kitchen, then get out of the safe house.

"I have to go, but I'll be in touch later, okay?" She was clearly trying to wrap up the call. "I promise everything is fine. Bye." She lowered the phone and ended the call. "I feel terrible not letting him know about the lake house incident."

"I know, but that would take a long explanation we don't have time for now." He took the phone from her fingers and set it on the kitchen table. "It will be easier news once we have the guy responsible behind bars."

"You're right." Her smile was weary. "To be honest, I can't wait for that to happen. For the danger to be over once and for all."

"I'm with you on that." He took one last glance around the safe house, then headed for the door. "Let's go. Aiden found a spot down the road between three evergreen trees that we can use for cover."

She nodded and followed him outside. Large puffy clouds had rolled in off Lake Michigan, providing some relief from the hot August sun. He didn't bother locking the door since there were several tactical team members and Finnegans stationed in various locations nearby keeping an eye out for anything remotely suspicious. By the time anyone resembling the arsonist approached the door, they'd be on top of him.

Rhy's team had earpiece radio devices that allowed them to communicate. Joe Kingsley, Rhy's team leader, had brought extras for the rest of them. Colin wasn't accustomed to hearing voices in his ear, but he did his best to listen to the chatter between the rest of the team while keeping alert for danger.

They walked down the street to the evergreen tree location. As they'd made plans, there had been a debate about evicting the neighbors. In the end, they'd agreed that with so many of them keeping watch, there shouldn't be any danger to the nearby properties. Kyleigh and Brady, would be set up closest to those properties, had agreed to evacuate those homes if something did go awry. He trusted his siblings to do that without a problem.

One thing about fire, it took a while to gain momentum. Even with an accelerant, the flames didn't spread instantaneously. Fire covered the area where the accelerant had been used, but the rest of the property would take time to burn.

Time enough to rescue anyone who might be in the houses nearby.

He and Faye stood near Aiden, nestled in the pine trees. Her gaze encompassed both of them. "How long do you think this will take?" Faye asked.

"No idea." Colin glanced through some of the thinner branches to see the road. "I have to assume it will take some time for this guy to realize your phone is on, then more time to locate and track it here. I've put everyone on alert about the sedan, but we should make sure to look at every vehicle approaching the property as a potential suspect." Colin wouldn't put anything past this guy, including stealing a car to throw them off track.

"You may as well sit down," Aiden advised. "We will likely be here for a while."

"I'm too nervous." Faye clasped her hands together. "I pray this guy shows up soon."

Colin knew it was very likely the arsonist wouldn't show up until dark, but he didn't say that. In his earpiece he could hear the guys warning each other to stay alert, emphasizing that waiting was the hardest part.

After ten minutes of standing, Faye dropped to the ground. She put her arms around her knees and rested her chin on them. "Maybe we should have waited until dark," she muttered.

"Maybe." He dropped down beside her. "I have faith that he'll show soon, though."

The chatter through the earpiece went silent as everyone settled in.

After fifteen minutes, Rhy's voice came through the earpiece. "Van approaching from the north, heading south."

"I see it," Joe Kingsley said. "Looks like two people in front."

Colin had given Aiden the binocs, which he used to zoom in on the van. "A young guy and a woman. Doubtful they're our target."

"Agreed. They're driving past," Brady said. "Final destination seems to be a house farther down the street."

"Roger that," Rhy confirmed.

They waited another hour without seeing anything out of the ordinary. Colin was beginning to doubt the wisdom of his plan. Granted, Rhy and the others had agreed, so he couldn't have been that far off base. This was their wheelhouse more so than his.

Still, the minutes dragged by with excruciating slowness.

"Another vehicle approaching from the south," Joe Kingsley said. "It's a dark-gray sedan."

Colin jumped to his feet. "Can I see?" he asked Aiden.

"Sure." His brother handed over the binocs. He found the sedan but couldn't get a good look at the driver. The angle of the sun caused a shadow. "I can't make out the driver's features," he muttered.

"The sedan is passing me," Kyleigh said a few minutes later. "The driver didn't slow down at all as he passed by."

"So maybe not our guy," Aiden said.

Colin knew there would likely be several false alarms before the arsonist showed. His stomach rumbled with hunger, but he ignored it.

"I see a kid walking down the street from the south," Joe said. "Wearing a baggy hoodie and a backpack over his shoulders. I don't see anything in either hand."

He thought about the kid on the boat and was about to take the binoculars when Faye took them. "I'd like to see."

He bit back a protest as she used the glasses to focus on the kid. She sucked in a harsh breath and shoved the binocs into his stomach. "It's Annie. We need to get her out of here!"

"Hold on—" But it was too late. Faye darted from the shelter of the trees, running straight toward her half sister.

Colin rushed after her, his stomach tied in knots. They were far from Brookland where Annie lived with Claire and Dorian Kimble.

What was she doing here?

CHAPTER FIFTEEN

"Annie!" Faye shouted to get her sister's attention. For a moment, she thought the teenager would ignore her, but then she stopped and waited for Faye to catch up. A strange smile creased her features.

"Fancy meeting you here, sis." Annie's tone reeked of sarcasm. She lifted her hand and flicked a lighter. On, then off. On and off.

A chill snaked down Faye's spine as realization sank deep into her bones. No, it couldn't be.

"Faye, stay back!" Colin's urgent tone came from behind her. "Don't go any closer. She might be armed."

"He's right." Annie's lips thinned in a grim smile. She opened her hoodie revealing a can of some sort tucked against her. Instantly, she had the can in one hand with the lighter in the other. "I am armed. This wasn't what I'd hoped to use, I have more in my backpack. But it will do in a pinch. It's time to end this once and for all."

"It was you?" Faye could barely comprehend what was happening. "You've been the one starting these fires? Why? What did I ever do to you?"

"You've been the golden girl for years," Annie hissed in a low, angry voice. "Dad has always loved you better than me. And you know what? He should love me more! I'm his real flesh-and-blood daughter, while you're just a stray kid he brought home and adopted from some lame family killed in a fire."

Faye gaped at her. "What are you talking about?"

"DNA," Annie spat. "Yours and mine. No genetic match. Not one little bit of shared DNA, which explains why you're so smart and I'm so dumb!" Annie was shouting now, her face contorted in a mask of rage.

Faye had no clue what Annie was talking about, although now that she thought about it, she didn't really resemble either of her parents. The DNA news was a shock, but that wasn't the pressing issue.

Talking her sister off the ledge was.

"You don't want to do this, Annie." Faye held her hands up, palms facing forward. As if that might stop the teenager from zapping her with accelerant and fire. "I never knew I wasn't my dad's biological daughter. You're incredibly smart to have figured that out."

"Don't patronize me!" Annie flicked the lighter on and off again. "I hate you!"

"I can understand how much you must resent me. But this isn't going to change anything, Annie. It will only hurt you. Please, don't do this. Hand the canister, lighter, and backpack to me, okay?" Faye continued talking to her in a calm voice, hoping and praying the Finnegans and the members of Rhy's tactical team could grab Annie without hurting her.

Or getting burned themselves.

"Stop it!" Annie's wide eyes looked wild. "I don't want to hear you talking!" She lifted the hand with the container and aimed it toward Faye as the other hand flicked the lighter.

"No!" Faye shouted. Colin ran forward, slapping Annie's hand holding the lighter upward. The lighter tumbled through the air, landing somewhere out of sight.

Colin slammed Annie against the ground, squashing the backpack beneath her. Instantly, the scent of lighter fluid enveloped them. Annie wrestled under Colin's weight, squirming as she tried to escape.

No, not escape. Faye watched as Annie pulled something out of the pocket of her jeans.

"She has another lighter!" She rushed forward to pull Colin off her sister just as Annie flicked the lighter on. The fluid must have leaked onto Annie's clothes, and Colin's too, because the flame raced along their damp clothing.

"No! Help!" Faye grabbed Colin, yanking hard to get him away from Annie. The rest of the Finnegans arrived, each of them tearing off their clothing, using the items to smother the flames.

"I hate you, I hate you, I hate you," Annie chanted as she fought off their attempts to rescue her. Colin stumbled upright, tore his paint-thinner-dampened shirt off, and tossed it aside.

"Are you hurt?" Faye raked her gaze over him.

"I'm okay. I wasn't as soaked as your sister."

The rest of the team was doing their best to put out the fire that engulfed Annie. Joe Kingsley raked the backpack off her and threw it into the center of the road a few yards away. "We need to get out of here," he shouted.

The group of Finnegans grabbed her sister and ran away from the backpack. Faye, Colin, and Rhy followed. There was a loud whooshing sound as the entire backpack ignited in a ball of fire.

"Annie, are you okay?" Reassured Colin had escaped the worst of the blaze, Faye turned her attention to Annie. Her sister had stopped screaming and chanting, likely overwhelmed now by the pain of the burn. "We need a first-aid kit."

"I've called 911," Kyleigh said, her expression grim. "They'll be here shortly."

Faye didn't like feeling helpless, but there wasn't anything she could do for her sister without medical supplies. Annie's left side, the hand she'd used to hold the canister, appeared to be the worst area of the burn. Maybe along her back, too, where she'd landed on the backpack.

"I'm sorry," Colin said in a low voice. "I heard her comment about having more in the backpack. I shouldn't have taken her down so hard and fast, but I was scared she'd hurt you."

"You have nothing to apologize for. My sister brought this upon herself." Faye still couldn't believe all these fires had been set by her sister. No wonder they'd been found at the lake house. And this also explained how her sister had been able to track her phone. They'd all used the find-my-phone app, especially when Annie was younger. She searched Colin's gaze. "Are you all right?"

"I think so." He glanced down at his bare chest. "I don't feel like I was burned that badly. Thanks to you, Faye. You pulled me off her right away."

"Not just me." She knew the quick response from the Finnegan family and Rhy's teammates had prevented Colin from being hurt too badly. Truly, Annie's injuries could have been worse too.

"You saved me," Colin said softly.

She wanted to lean against him, soak up his strength. "We saved each other." Before she could say anything more, wailing sirens split the air. Annie's backpack was still a burning mass in the center of the road when the firetrucks and ambulance arrived.

Faye rushed over to help herself to the ambulance supplies while giving orders. "I'm Dr. Kimble from the Trinity ED. This is my sister, Annie Kimble. You need to take her to Trinity's burn center ASAP. I want her to get the best burn care possible."

"You got it, Dr. Kimble." The EMTs did not hesitate to place Annie's gurney in the back. Her sister was sobbing now, crying out in pain. Faye hated hearing the agony in her sister's voice but didn't jump in to join her. For one thing, she didn't want to cause her sister any more distress. Not after the hatred she'd spewed. Better for her to meet up with Annie at the hospital later, but in the meantime, she needed to provide care to Colin and call her dad.

He'd be devastated over this. And so would Claire. Annie was in deep, deep trouble. Larry had died because of her fire. And others had been put in harm's way too. She'd burned a car and two homes. Not to mention attempted murder.

Many felony charges would be brought against her. And Annie was only sixteen!

She forced herself to turn away. "Colin, I need to see your arms and chest."

He held his arms out from his sides in a move that would have made her smile under less grim circumstances. She could see there were a few areas of pink skin and one area in particular where the hairs had been singed away, much like the wound on his arm. The gauze wrap had protected his one extremity, but now she had the other to worry about too. She used a bottle of sterile water to soak the gauze, then pressed them against the worst areas on his torso and bare arm.

"We'll need to take you to the hospital, Colin. No arguments this time." She glanced at Rhy. "I'll also need my phone from the safe house so I can contact my dad. He'll want to get to the hospital to see Annie."

"I'm sorry things ended this way." Rhy's empathetic expression warmed her heart.

"Me too." She swallowed hard and squared her shoulders. "I want to thank all of you for your help with this. If I had known about Annie . . ." She couldn't finish.

"I'll grab your phone." Kyleigh ran off, returning a few minutes later. She grimaced as she handed it over. "I guess our ruse worked."

"Yeah." Faye knew this scenario could have ended far worse.

"Come on, we'll get Colin to Trinity," Aiden said firmly. "I'm sure Mitch will want to talk to us, too, once Colin has been cared for."

She nodded and followed Aiden and Colin to one of the Finnegans' vehicles. She'd lost track of which belonged to whom.

As they headed to Trinity, she stared down at her phone for a long moment before calling her dad. The danger was over, but the nightmare wasn't. If anything, she felt more depressed than before. It was one thing to know a stranger wanted to kill you.

But to find out how much your own sister hated you? Enough to set you on fire? That was worse.

Granted, Annie was only a teenager. She'd need both medical and psychiatric care. More of the latter, Faye knew, based on how unhinged she'd been during all of this. Regardless, their small family would be forever fractured.

Never to be the same again.

COLIN FELT terrible about how he'd botched things outside the safe house. But the moment he'd seen the teenager's intent to spray Faye with the accelerant and light her on fire, he'd lost it. If he'd thought to pull his weapon, he'd have shot her without hesitation.

Instead, he'd gotten her burned.

"Dad? It's Faye. I'm afraid I have some bad news." He listened as Faye described the incident outside the safe house. She'd kept it brief but had ended the call with, "Annie needs you and Claire to be there. So please, hurry."

He could only imagine how Chief Kimble felt about having an arsonist daughter. Worse, she'd set so many fires damaging so much property and ultimately killing Larry that he didn't see how the teenager would escape prosecution. Maybe if the state didn't try her as an adult, she wouldn't spend the rest of her life in prison.

Taking Faye's hand, he said, "Do you think her DNA comments are true?"

"I don't know." Faye sighed and glanced at him. "In a way, it makes sense. I never resembled my parents much. But even if it's true, I don't understand why she grew to hate me. We barely interacted over these past few years. I babysat her when she was younger, but that stopped when I entered college, then medical school."

"It's strange that she'd harbor so much animosity toward you." Colin searched her gaze. There was so much he wanted to tell her, but this didn't seem the time or the place.

"She needs help," Faye whispered. "Professional help."

Colin silently agreed. Aiden pulled up in front of the

emergency department at Trinity Medical Center. He slid out of the car and walked inside with Faye beside him, resigning himself to a long wait.

Faye wasn't having that, though, using her clout as a doc to get him into a room within ten minutes. He felt a little guilty skipping to the head of the line.

"You shouldn't have done that." He glanced around. "I'm not that bad."

"I want your wounds cared for properly." She surprised him by taking his hand in hers. "I care about you. Watching Annie grab another lighter to burn you was the worst thing I'd ever witnessed."

"Hey, I'm okay." He wanted to draw her close, but the skin on his chest was feeling a bit raw. Like a bad sunburn when he and his sibs had played sand volleyball on Bradford Beach. "I'm fine. And you were the one she wanted to hurt. I'm so sorry we never thought of her as a possible suspect. So much for most arsonists being young men."

"That possibility never occurred to me either." She stared down at their joined hands. "I wonder if she borrowed the motor scooter from her friend, the one she was supposedly spending the weekend with." She paused, then added, "The sedan is hers, the one my father bought for her. She had everything, Colin, but it wasn't enough."

"Try not to dwell on that," he murmured. Although he couldn't imagine any of the Finnegans turning on their own.

She sighed. "At least the danger is over now. I don't know how to thank you. The support you've provided over these past few days has been amazing."

"I care about you." He hesitated, wondering how much more he should tell her. A physician entered the room, interrupting them.

Over the next fifteen to twenty minutes, the medical

team cleaned and dressed his burns. They removed the bandage to his arm that Faye had applied, replacing it with a fresh one.

"You'll need to keep these clean and dry for the next two weeks," the doc informed him. "No getting the bandages wet, and I want the dressings changed twice daily."

"I think I can manage that." He was relieved the burns weren't as bad as he'd feared.

"I'll help you," Faye offered.

"Here's a note stating you will need to be off work for the next two weeks." The doc handed him a slip of paper, then smiled at Faye. "With Dr. Kimble keeping an eye on your wounds, I don't think you need to follow up with your regular doctor. But if they change in any way, get worse or look infected, then please come back right away."

"I will," he promised. It was nice to know Faye wanted to watch over him. Although he wished he knew if she'd offered out of a sense of obligation or from something more personal.

There was only one way to find out.

"Faye." He reached out to take both of her hands in his. "I want you to know—"

"Colin!" Alanna burst into the room interrupting him. "Why didn't you tell me you were here?" His sister's eyes widened when she saw Faye. "Dr. Kimble? You're not on duty tonight. Why are you here?"

He sighed, knowing his sister would nag until she'd learned the truth. "Alanna, I've been helping to keep Faye safe. I suffered some minor burns as a result of a tussle with an arsonist." He glanced down at the bandages on his chest. "I'm fine, though, nothing more than two small areas of second-degree burns."

"Burns! Did you get that on the job?" Alanna frowned. "No, that's impossible. Your gear would have protected you."

"It's my fault," Faye said. "The arsonist was after me, but Colin jumped directly into danger to protect me."

Alanna's jaw dropped, her gaze bouncing between him and Faye. "Why do I think there's more to this story?"

"I can fill you in later." Colin slid off the gurney, trying to think of a way to get rid of his sister. "You should get back to your patients who need you, Alanna. I promise I'm fine."

His sister sighed. "Hold on. I'll grab you a scrub top. You can't go walking around shirtless." Alanna left as abruptly as she'd barged in.

He turned to take Faye's hands in his, hoping the second time was the charm. "Faye, I lo—"

"Faye? I've been looking all over for you." Chief Kimble's voice boomed from the doorway. Whatever happened to patient privacy? His room was getting more traffic than the Marquette freeway interchange during rush hour.

"Dad." Faye slipped her hands from his, turning to face her father. "I'm sorry."

Chief Kimble wrapped Faye in his arms, giving Colin a solemn nod. "Nothing for you to be sorry about. I owe Colin here a debt of gratitude for keeping you safe. And if anyone should apologize, it's me. I'm the one who has failed Annie."

"You didn't fail her, I'm the one she hated." Faye stepped back to look up at her father. "I had no idea she resented me so much. I want to go check on her, but I'm not sure she'll want to see me."

"Claire is with her," Dorian said. "There is one large third-degree burn on her back. Sounds like she'll need surgery—" His voice broke. The large man lifted his hand to pinch the bridge of his nose, taking a moment to pull himself together. Colin averted his gaze, feeling bad for what the older guy was going through. "She also needs psychiatric help," Dorian finally added. "Claire is determined to hire the best lawyer possible to prevent Annie from serving a lengthy prison term."

Faye nodded. "I think that's smart. She needs help, Dad. And I'm willing to do my part if that helps. Family counseling or whatever."

He nodded. "I heard she told you the truth. About how your mother and I adopted you thirty years ago."

"Yes. But it's okay, I'm not angry or anything." Faye grimaced. "Maybe a little upset you didn't tell me sooner."

"Your entire family perished in the fire," Dorian said. "If there was any chance of reuniting you with your blood family, I wouldn't have kept the secret. But they were gone, and your mother had just suffered a miscarriage." He managed a smile. "We both gratefully accepted the chance to adopt you."

Now that father and daughter were standing side by side, Colin could see what Faye meant about not looking like her parents. He didn't say anything, unwilling to interrupt.

"I'm surprised you were able to keep it a secret," Faye murmured.

"Only because there wasn't much social media thirty years ago. These days keeping that quiet would be impossible." Dorian's expression sobered. "I'm sorry if that caused you to be upset."

"It didn't. I'm blessed to have had a wonderful life with you and Mom." Faye hugged him again. "I think you should go offer your support to Claire and Annie now. They'll need your strength to get through this."

"I will." Dorian kissed the top of her head, then stepped around Faye, holding out his hand to Colin. "Thank you again, Colin. I appreciate everything you've done for my daughter."

"You're welcome, sir." He somberly shook Chief Kimble's hand.

"I hope those injuries won't keep you off the job too long." The older man frowned as if first noticing the dressings. "We need more men like you in the ranks, Finnegan."

"Two weeks, sir," Colin admitted. "But I'll be back as soon as possible after that."

Chief Dorian nodded, then turned back to face his daughter. "I'll let you know about Annie's condition when I learn more. For now, you should head home to get some rest. And you're welcome to stay at our place."

"Ah, thanks. I'll let you know." Faye's evasive response told Colin she didn't want to go there. And he couldn't blame her. Not after everything that had happened.

As the chief left, Alanna returned with a scrub top. "Here. Do you need help putting it on?"

"I can dress myself, thanks." He took the green scrub top and bit back a wince as he lifted it up and over his arms and head. He walked over to stand beside Faye. "We should get out of here. I'm sure there are other patients who need this bed more than I do."

"I'm going to hold you to your promise," Alanna called out after him. "I want to hear the whole story, Colin."

He lifted a hand acknowledging her comment but kept walking. Twice he'd tried to tell Faye how much he loved her.

And he'd been interrupted both times. He led the way through the hospital waiting room, then outside. When they were a few steps from the entrance, he turned to Faye. "I was wondering if you would be willing to stay in my guest room for a few nights. I won't invade your privacy or anything, but I could tell you didn't really want to bunk with your father and stepmother. Besides, you would be doing me a favor in helping with my dressings."

"Your guest room?" She searched his gaze as if to ferret out the truth behind his offer. He'd never taken advantage of the situation when they'd been hiding from Annie and wasn't about to start now.

"I was only trying to offer an alternate place for you to stay. There's plenty of room at the homestead too. I know Rhy, Devon, Quinn, Sami, Aiden, and Elly won't mind putting you up for a while. Whatever you're most comfortable with works for me."

She took a step closer to him. "Given my options, I'd rather stay with you, Colin." She rested her hand above his chest wound near his heart. "I know things have been rough, but I care about you, very much. To be honest, I had a crush on you in high school."

"You did?" He was shocked by her admission. "Why didn't I know that? I wanted to ask you to prom, but you took the wind out of my sails when you graduated at the end of December so you could attend college."

She smiled. "Attending college early seemed like a good idea at the time. I was anxious to get out of the house. But, Colin? If you had asked me to the prom, I would have said yes."

"Ah, Faye." He pulled her closer, gently so as not to put undue pressure on his injury. "I've spent the last ten minutes trying to tell you how much I love you. I know we'll need to take things slow, your family has to come first. But I want to be there for you."

"I love you too, Colin." She lifted up on her tiptoes to

kiss him. "If I had known what real love felt like, I never would have married Rory."

"It's not up to us to question God's plan," he murmured. "I guess we both had to go through some difficult times in order to be here together."

"I hadn't considered that. I spent too much time wondering why God let me make such a foolish mistake."

"I love you, Faye. Let's not worry about the past. Not when we have a bright future ahead of us." He kissed her again, glad they'd finally had a few minutes to themselves. Even if they were standing outside a very busy emergency department.

"There you are," Aiden said from behind them. "Oops. My bad. Am I interrupting?"

Colin broke off the kiss and rested his forehead against Faye's for a moment before turning to glare at his brother. "Yeah. You are. Beat it, kid."

"Good one. You used to tell me that all the time when we were young." Aiden snickered and shook his head. "I didn't listen then, what makes you think I'll listen now?"

"Be nice," Faye whispered. "We need him to drive us home."

He stifled a groan. "Fine. Aiden, will you please drive us home?"

"Sure." His younger brother flashed a grin. "Who's home exactly?"

"Mine." Colin lifted a hand. "Don't give Faye any grief. Her house is nothing but a burned shell. She needs a place to stay, and my guest room is as good as any."

"Me? Give you grief? I wouldn't dream of it." The teasing glint in his brother's eyes gave him away. "I'm sure you'll hear from Rhy and Tarin soon enough."

Of course, he would. Faye stepped back, so he caught

her hand in his. "Aiden, why don't you go get the car? We'll wait here."

"What, you're an invalid now?" Aiden snorted, then pulled the keys from his pocket. "Fine. I'll be here shortly."

When his brother jogged across to the grassy area toward the parking structure, he pulled Faye in close again. "I love you, Faye. I hope you don't let my family scare you off. I know they can be overbearing at times. They're pretty much professionals at sticking their noses in where they don't belong."

"I love your family, Colin." She smiled up at him. "Almost as much as I love you."

"Good." He kissed her again, basking in her love. He wasn't sure what he'd ever done to deserve her, but now that he had Faye as a part of his life?

He'd never let her go.

EPILOGUE

Four weeks later . . .

Faye stood beside Colin, gazing at the demolition in progress. Her house had been so badly damaged that her insurance company had suggested pulling down what was left and starting over. They had given her a very fair settlement, more than enough to rebuild.

Or put a nice down payment on another property. She could sell the lot once the debris of her old house had been removed. She was leaning toward buying something else. A fresh start sounded good.

"Are you sorry to see it go?" Colin asked.

"No." She tried to find the words to explain. "I don't miss the house. It feels as if that was part of my old life. I have a new life now with you."

"Aw, Faye. You say the sweetest things." He gave her a quick kiss, then turned her toward his SUV. "Let's go. We have another stop to make before we head home."

"Another stop?" She slid into the passenger seat, watching him warily. "It's Saturday, not Sunday, so we can't be going to the homestead."

"Not today." He grinned and started the engine. "You'll see."

She decided not to argue but sat back to enjoy the ride. Mitch had discovered Jayson Sanders had visited his buddy in Florida and was planning to take a firefighter position down there. All along they'd been focused on the wrong man, and she'd felt a bit guilty over thinking the worst about him.

But that was in the past. She needed to concentrate on the present. The fall weather was turning cooler, which she liked. This was their second weekend off in a row as they'd attended Quinn and Sami's wedding the weekend before. It had been a small, sweet, and intimate affair. No big cere-mony with loads of people attending, the way her first wedding had been. She'd liked how the Finnegans didn't do things to be showy or draw undue attention. They seemed to know that marriage was more than pomp and circumstance.

It was a solemn commitment to spending the rest of your life together.

The last four weeks had been hectic. More so for her family. Annie had undergone several surgeries to the large third-degree burn to her back. And she was still in the hospital being cared for by a skilled burn team and psychi-atry too. She'd visited Annie once, and her sister had gotten so upset she hadn't stayed long.

At this point, the ADA assigned to her case, Maddy Sinclair, who happened to be Mitch Callahan's sister, had held off pressing charges. Annie's lawyer claimed Annie wasn't competent to stand trial and in her sister's current position, that was true. The plan was to wait until Annie had recovered at least physically from her burn care.

Emotionally and psychologically, Faye wasn't sure if her sister would ever fully recover.

Her dad and Claire had attended several counseling sessions too. They were doing better, although Faye still felt animosity from Claire. As if it was Faye's fault Annie had gone off the deep end. Somehow Annie had gotten fixated on all of Faye's successes and used that as a reason to think less of herself.

In contrast, the Finnegan family had embraced her with open arms. Every last one of them had treated her like she belonged. Especially Elly, the youngest of the group. Elly greeted her with a big hug every time she and Colin attended family dinner.

"We're heading downtown?" She guessed after they'd been on the road for several minutes.

"Yes. To the beach." Colin searched her gaze for a moment. "I thought it was time to make some new memories. In new places."

They'd gone to Brookland Park shortly after Colin's burns had healed, but the place wasn't the same since the fire. The women's room door had been repaired, but the new door alongside the scorched brick served as a reminder of how she'd suffered smoke inhalation.

Yeah, she didn't find the solace she used to in Brookland Park. But she always experienced a sense of peace when she was with Colin. The sun was still bright in the sky when they reached the lakefront. She took Colin's hand as they strolled along the shoreline. When they reached an area away from the other beachgoers, Colin turned and went down on one knee.

"Faye, will you please marry me?" He pulled a velvet box from his pocket, opened it, and removed a diamond engagement ring. "I asked your father for permission to marry you, and he gave us his blessing."

"You did? Really?" That was something Rory hadn't done. Her eyes misted with tears. Happy, joyful tears as she held out her hand for him to slip the ring on her finger. "Yes, Colin. I'd be honored to marry you. I love you and your family very much."

"And we love you too. Well, me more so than the rest of them." He chuckled, surged to his feet, and enveloped her in a big hug. "I'd like to put my condo up for sale so that we can find a new place to live, together."

"I'd love that," she admitted.

"Good." His grin widened. "Thanks for making me the happiest man in the world."

"I want a small wedding just like Quinn and Sami's," she warned.

"Fine with me. I don't need anything fancy." He leaned back and shouted, "She loves me!"

"He loves me too!" she shouted back.

Colin's exuberance was contagious, and soon they were laughing and swirling in dance moves along the sandy beach. Her heart had been heavy with sadness for Annie, her father, and Claire, but today?

Today she could feel the Lord's blessing shining from above, enveloping them with hope and love.

Especially love.

I HOPE you enjoyed Colin and Faye's story in *Scorched Secrets*. I'm having a blast with the Finnegans and their Callahan cousins. Are you ready for Alanna and Reed's story in *Critical Response*? Click here!

DEAR READER

I'm a little sad that I'm over halfway finished with the series! I've enjoyed the Finnegan family, especially the way these noble men and women put their lives on the line to save the innocent. And it's been wonderful to bring in the Callahans too. For those of you who enjoyed my Callahan Confidential series, you'll love catching up with members of the family as they cross paths and support the Finnegans. And you know there will be a large family reunion at the end.

If you enjoyed Colin and Faye's story in *Scorched Secrets*, take a moment to check out *Critical Response*, Alanna and Reed's story. Anyone choosing to purchase any eBooks or audiobooks (including these new Finnegan stories) directly from my website will receive a 15% discount by using the code **LauraScott15**.

I adore hearing from my readers! I can be found through my website at https://www.laurascottbooks.com, via Facebook at https://www.facebook.com/LauraScott Books, Instagram at https://www.instagram.com/laurascott books/, and Twitter https://twitter.com/laurascottbooks.

Also, take a moment to sign up for my monthly newsletter to learn about my new book releases! All subscribers receive a free novella not available for purchase on any platform.

Until next time,

Laura Scott

CRITICAL RESPONSE

Chapter One

"Alanna, you're up for the ambo patient slotted for room three."

Alanna Finnegan nodded to indicate she'd heard the charge nurse's directive as she finished typing her discharge note. No surprise that she'd discharged one patient barely two minutes ago, and the next one was already on the way. Beds in the emergency department rarely grew cold between patients. October wasn't as busy as summertime, but the nice weather had lingered, keeping the influx of patients steady.

Truthfully, she'd rather be busy during her twelve-hour shifts.

One thing for sure, this job was never boring. Her feet ached from the miles she put on every shift, but she didn't mind. When she'd finished at the computer, she stood and glanced up at the census board. Now that the hospital's ED was computerized, names of their incoming patients automatically populated the screen thanks to the dispatcher working in the paramedic base. Her new admission was a twenty-three-year-old man named Ivan Garcia. And no surprise, his presenting problem was a gunshot wound to the thigh.

Trinity Medical Center was the only level one trauma center in the city of Milwaukee. As such, the paramedic base was set up in a small room near the emergency department. There were two level one trauma centers in the entire state, the second one being in Madison. The nursing staff with their gallows humor described those patients with gunshot or knife wounds as playing in the knife and gun club. Not that the injuries were always their fault, innocent people could be victims of crimes. But she had enough experience to know the innocent victims were in the less than 15 percent category. The other 85 percent were generally not so innocent and therefore accompanied by Milwaukee police officers when they were injured during the commission of a crime.

Ivan's injury must not have been serious enough to require a trip to the trauma bay. Her patient would be there any moment, so she peeked inside to make sure the room had been cleaned. Carin Graves, their housekeeper, was good about being on top of things. Thankfully, she'd been in and out in record time, and the room sparkled. Since she wasn't sure if the patient's bullet would need to be removed, she set up a surgical tray on a table in the corner just in case. She deftly unwrapped the tray, while leaving the clear plastic covering to keep the instruments sterile, so that they were readily accessible.

Thirty seconds later, the ambulance bay doors burst open. Two EMTs wheeled a gurney through the opening. No police officer was in attendance, indicating the patient was not in custody. Which was probably a good thing. It didn't really matter to her one way or the other, she treated her patients equally regardless of their guilt or innocence.

"Twenty-three-year-old male suffering a gunshot wound to the right thigh. His vitals are stable," the female paramedic said as they pushed the gurney into the room. "Bullet is still embedded in the thigh muscle, though, and we've packed the wound with gauze."

"Thanks." Together, they moved Ivan Garcia from the ambulance gurney to the bed using the sheet beneath him to slide him over. The EMTs wheeled the cart out of the room, drawing the privacy curtain closed behind them. Their job of transporting the patient was over.

This young man was her patient now. She smiled down at him as she pulled her stethoscope from around her neck. Despite the fact that there were no police officers in attendance, she couldn't help noticing the three red teardrops tattooed down his face from the corner of his right eye. She knew gangs used that specific tattoo to boast about killing people, one teardrop for each person. Three in Ivan's case. Averting her gaze, she reminded herself that this guy was twenty-three. He could have done the deed years ago; she'd seen similar tattoos on fifteen-year-old kids. "Ivan, my name is Alanna. I'll be your nurse for the next two hours." Her shift officially ended at seven thirty in the evening, but she often had to stay later to help keep the patients flowing in and out of the ED. "How are you feeling?"

"How do you think?" Ivan scowled. "I've been shot."

She nodded, her gaze sympathetic. "I know, I'm sorry. How is your thigh pain?"

"Bad." He pinned her with a narrow gaze. "Ten out of ten." The way he'd used the pain score of ten out of ten made her think he was no stranger to being in the hospital. Had he been admitted with other injuries? Once she had a chance to look into his electronic medical record, she'd know more. But she couldn't help but think those blood red teardrops had been inked on his skin more recently than she'd thought. A twinge of unease niggled at the back of her neck. She did her best to ignore it.

"Okay, I'll check with the doctor to see if he'll order you some pain medication. First, though, I need to listen to your heart and lungs and take a set of vital signs." His heartbeat was strong, his lungs clear. She took his blood pressure, noting the higher reading likely due to his pain, then removed the cuff from his arm. "We need to have you connected to our heart monitor, okay?"

She turned to grab the EKG patches from the package behind her, intending to place them on his chest. Before she could do anything, her patient abruptly rolled off the gurney and grabbed her from behind. He brought his arm across her neck, pressing tightly against her throat in a vice-like grip.

She was so surprised by his actions she didn't have time to scream. With his arm choking her, breathing was impossible too.

Help, she silently shouted.

"You're going to get me outta here before the cops show up, understand?" The harsh voice in her ear was punctuated by a tightening of his arm around her neck. He reeked of sweat and alcohol. Anxious to appease him, she nodded.

Ivan dragged her several feet across the room before she could get her bearings. No! This couldn't be happening! Remembering his thigh wound, she tried to wiggle into a better position to use his injury to escape.

She hadn't grown up with six older brothers without learning some self-defense.

Ivan stopped near the curtain as if understanding there would be plenty of other staff members outside the room. She used his momentary pause to her advantage, lifting her right leg and kicking backward at his injured thigh and knee with all her strength. Her rubber-soled shoes wouldn't normally do much damage, but somehow she managed to hit her target.

Ivan howled in pain, but his grip around her neck didn't loosen. If anything, it tightened painfully. He reached out toward the surgical tray and poked his fingers through the plastic to grab the scalpel. "Do that again and I'll slice your throat, understand?" His voice was low and harsh in her ear. Smelling his foul breath, she fought the urge to gag. "I'm not going back to jail!"

Alanna froze when she felt the sharp edge of the blade cutting into the skin beneath her chin. Warm blood trickled down her neck, running over his arm still locked around her throat.

Why had she set up the surgical tray? She inwardly railed at herself for being so foolish, even though it was too late for regrets now.

"We're walking out of here." He twisted his body to use his shoulder to shove the privacy curtain aside. He dragged her through the opening, and at first, no one paid them any attention.

People came in and out of rooms all the time. She tried to call out but could only make a croaking sound.

It was enough to have one of her nurse colleagues, Dana Callahan, glance over. Her eyes widened when she saw the arm across Alanna's throat and the blood staining her neck. "Hey, what are you doing?"

"Stay back or I'll kill her!" Ivan's voice echoed through the area. The ED was set up in teams, and they were in the orange team, which was closest to the red team formerly known as the trauma bay.

Dana, Dr. Willis, and even the housekeeper Carin's expressions all reflected surprise and horror. They simply stood there, gaping in shock as Ivan held the blade to her throat. She couldn't really blame them. She doubted she'd have reacted much differently.

Alanna wanted to kick at Ivan's injured leg again, but she feared the blade of the scalpel was too close to her jugular vein or worse her carotid artery. One deep swipe and she could easily bleed out before anyone could save her.

Please, Lord Jesus, keep us all safe!

A sense of calmness washed over her. Ivan wanted her for a reason. His plan was to escape being questioned by the police. All gunshot and knife wounds were an automatic report to the cops. By playing along, she could buy time.

There was a Milwaukee County sheriff's deputy stationed in the waiting room of the emergency department to help deal with family members of patients who were in police custody. An unfortunately common occurrence. Someone would call him or her in to help.

Wouldn't they?

Her patient continued dragging her step by step toward the ambulance bay doors. Her ID badge was dislodged from her scrubs, dropping to the floor, the hard plastic making a soft noise as it hit the linoleum and skated across the floor.

"Hey, you need to let Alanna go." Doctor Willis, the attending physician assigned to the orange team, stepped forward, concern etched in his features. "You want to leave without receiving medical care and treatment? That's fine with us. But kidnapping a staff member is going to bring all kinds of trouble raining down on you."

"Stay back!" Ivan shouted, dragging her closer to the ambulance bay doors. "I won't hesitate to kill her!"

Alanna wanted to believe it was an empty threat, but the sharp edge of the blade convinced her otherwise. The three red teardrops inked on his face flashed in her memory. He'd killed before, and she understood he wouldn't hesitate to kill again. She tried to swallow past the forearm pressed against her throat. Her inability to breathe normally was making her dizzy.

How long before she passed out?

Not long.

Her foot tangled with the legs of a chair as Ivan continued dragging her past the row of rooms. The blade dug deeper into her neck. Tears pricked her eyes as she struggled to stay upright and focused. Surely, he'd let her go once they were outside.

And if he didn't?

He might decide to kill her. Why? She had no idea.

Her gaze stumbled across a tall dark-haired man wearing a dark uniform moving between the staff members. She easily recognized him as police officer Reed Carmichael. He worked out of the Fifth Precinct and often accompanied patients to the emergency department. Had in fact done that very thing yesterday during their respective shifts.

His blue eyes were locked on hers as he edged closer, using the staff as camouflage. His gaze silently promised he was there to rescue her.

Looking into Reed's eyes made her relax. She'd gotten to know him over the busy summer months and trusted him almost as much as she did her cop brothers.

"Stop where you are, pig!" Ivan shouted. "One step closer and I'll cut her throat."

Reed stopped partially behind Dr. Willis. Alanna had hoped Ivan wouldn't notice Reed's approach, but the guy's survival instincts had been honed to a sharp edge, much like the scalpel at her throat.

Ivan pulled her closer to the ambulance bay doors, leaving her little choice but to go along with him. She'd hoped he would let her go once they were outside, but now she wasn't sure that was Ivan's intent at all.

The ambulance doors opened, and two more men stepped through the doorway. She couldn't see them but heard Ivan's grunt as if he'd expected to have assistance.

No! They were going to take her with them!

A gunshot rang out. The arm around her throat loosened. She gasped for breath, dropping to the floor as Ivan's body fell backward. Blood ran freely down her neck from where the scalpel blade had sliced along her skin.

"Alanna!" Her name was a strangled sound as Reed ran toward her. She stared up at him for a moment before everything went dark.

"WHERE'S THE DOC?" Reed Carmichael cradled Alanna Finnegan in his arms on the floor, glancing frantically toward the hospital staff. "Her throat has been cut!"

A physician and a dark-haired nurse named Dana came running over. The doc's expression turned grim. "I don't think he hit the artery, but we need to get her into room three."

Knowing the general layout of the emergency department, Reed didn't hesitate to scoop Alanna into his arms. He strode to room three. The bed was messy, making him realize this must have been the room the perp had been in.

It wasn't ideal, but this was likely the only empty room they had. He gently set her on the bed, then forced himself to step back, giving Dana and the doc room to work.

Reed's heart thundered against his ribs as the medical team tended to Alanna. She was in good hands, so he turned away to head back over to where Ivan Garcia, a.k.a. Ice, was lying dead on the hospital floor. There was blood everywhere, Alanna's and Ivan's. He glanced toward the ambulance doors, but the two men who'd stepped through earlier were gone now. As much as he wanted to track them down, he couldn't leave the scene of an officer-involved shooting.

Especially when he was the officer in question.

Taking out a perp was bad enough, but doing so in the middle of a hospital emergency department was worse. He could already hear the MPD upper brass and hospital administrators screaming about this.

And he understood, this never should have happened. Where in the world was Wesley Durango, the rookie cop who'd offered to accompany Ice to the hospital? The shooting scene had been chaotic, but he'd thought the rookie had jumped up into the ambulance with their wounded perp.

Yet if he had, there was no sign of Durango now.

Reed half expected the rookie to have gone to find a cup of coffee or something as equally ridiculous. Yet that didn't change the fact that Durango should have had Ivan Garcia cuffed to the bed.

Sheriff's Deputy Mike Callahan came rushing in from the waiting room, accompanied by a woman in a suit, clearly someone from the C suite. "What happened?" Mike asked.

Reed glanced at the hospital administrator. Her name

badge identified her as Kathy Tusk, Vice President of Hospital Operations.

This was the beginning of his interrogation, one that would start with the hospital administrators and continue through the internal affairs division of the Milwaukee Police Department. He gestured toward the dead man. "This is Ivan Garcia, a.k.a. Ice. He's a high ranking member of the Blood Kings, a well-known drug gang."

"You shot him in the hospital?" Tusk demanded. "What were you thinking?"

"He held one of your nurses hostage with a scalpel blade to her neck. I had to stop him before he dragged her from the building." He glanced at Mike Callahan. "There were two other gang members who came in through the ambulance doors. We need all the video surveillance of the incident so we can get their pictures out to every cop on the street."

"You'll need a warrant to get the video," Tusk snapped.

Reed tamped down his anger. This woman acted as if she was more concerned about his shooting of a gang member than she was about her own staff member. "I'm sure you'll want to check in on Alanna Finnegan, she's being treated for the cut in her neck in room three."

Tusk paled and spun away to see for herself. Mike sent him a sympathetic glance. "Have you called this in?"

"Not yet." He lifted his hand to his radio to make the call. The minute he said the words *officer-involved shooting*, he'd heard the dispatcher suck in a harsh breath and knew there would be dozens of cops there within minutes. He released the radio and sighed. "The worst part is that I'll be placed on administrative leave."

"I know. That's a bummer." Mike clapped him on the

shoulder. "Good shooting, though. I'm glad you saved my cousin's life."

"Your cousin?" He glanced back toward Alanna's room. "I didn't realize you were related."

"We only found out earlier this year." Mike's expression turned serious. "That was a close call. How did he get a weapon in the first place?"

"It must have been in the room. I'm sure there are plenty of scalpels and other sharp objects here that can be turned against the staff." Reed rubbed the back of his neck, feeling the weight of his actions bearing down on him. The upper brass would watch whatever video was available and interview witnesses, dissecting everything he'd done or hadn't done. It was difficult at times to make administrators understand how fast a situation could unravel.

The second he'd seen the two additional gang members coming inside, he'd been forced to use deadly force to save Alanna's life. The three of them would have gotten her outside and likely killed her if he hadn't.

Knowing his time in the ED was limited, he walked back toward Alanna's room. Her eyes were open now, and there was a gauze bandage over the cut in her throat. The doc was explaining about the stitches that would need to be placed to close the wound, reassuring her that they'd have a plastic surgeon do the work to minimize a scar.

Alanna's gaze shifted from the doctor to him. Her dark-brown eyes shone with gratitude as they clung to his. He wanted to push past everyone to reach her bedside and take her hand. To assure her she'll never be hurt like that again.

But he didn't. Pounding footsteps indicated his backup had arrived. He turned to see several cops rushing in through the ambulance bay doors, stopping abruptly upon seeing the perp lying dead on the floor.

Yeah, this would not be fun. When Sergeant Noah Sinclair walked in, he headed straight toward him. He offered his weapon, butt first, then unclipped his badge and handed that over as well. Sinclair took both items, dropping them into an evidence bag.

"What happened?" Noah Sinclair was known to be a fair and decent boss. He didn't sit behind the desk like some of the older guys but preferred being out in the field. Reed also knew Noah was Mike Callahan's brother-in-law; he was married to Maddy who worked for the DA's office.

Reed was surprised to note that the rookie wasn't among those who'd come rushing to the hospital. Where was he? He turned his attention to Noah. "I take full responsibility, Sarg. I thought Wes accompanied this perp to the emergency department, but he didn't." He and several other cops had been dealing with rival gang members who had been armed.

Noah grimaced but nodded. "I'll talk to him. What happened here?"

Reed filled him in on how Ivan "Ice" Garcia had taken Alanna as a hostage by holding a scalpel to her neck. "I don't know what he intended, but it could be that he wanted her to provide medical care to his gunshot wound outside the hospital."

"Alanna Finnegan?" Noah sighed. "Great, we'll be hearing from her brothers Rhy and Tarin any minute."

"I know." The Finnegan family had gotten some press over the past several months, especially with Tarin being a detective and Rhy being captain of the tactical unit. Alanna had mentioned her family during one of their brief conversations. And now he could add the Callahans into the mix. As if having siblings in law enforcement wasn't enough, there were cousins too. "Ice was dragging Alanna toward the door. When two gang members showed up, I had little choice but to shoot him, taking him out of the picture to save Alanna's life. Unfortunately, that sent the other gang members running. We may get something off the hospital video on their ride, which could lead us to them."

"Do you think they wanted something more than nursing care from Alanna?" Noah asked.

He shrugged. "Anything is possible, but how would Ice know Alanna would be assigned as his nurse? At the most, he may have known she was working today, but even that wouldn't be easy to find out. Not unless he knew someone working inside the hospital. Besides, I don't think he'd shoot himself on purpose to get here." The more he thought about it, the less he believed this to be a personal attack against Alanna. "I was on scene when the drug deal went south. Ice was shot by a rival gang member from the Latino Hombres. I think his grabbing Alanna had been a spur of the moment decision."

"Yeah, okay." Noah glanced around at the chaotic scene in the emergency department. "This will be a nightmare."

"Tell me about it." Reed didn't think there was anything he could have done differently. Other than making sure that idiot Wesley did his job in accompanying Ice to the hospital.

The rookie's absence concerned him. "Sarg, I haven't seen Wes Durango since we responded to the scene of the initial shooting. He hasn't shown up here yet."

Noah's scowl deepened as he used his radio to contact the rookie. There was a long pause as Sinclair waited.

No response.

A shiver of unease slid down his spine. Without hesitation, Reed ran through the ambulance bay doors and into the cool autumn air. He took his time searching each of the squads that were parked all along the front of the emergency department.

Where was the rookie?

Reed's gaze dropped to the squad he'd driven here. He'd purposefully left it parked near the multilevel concrete parking garage. He frowned when he noticed someone was in the passenger seat.

Wesley? That was odd because Reed had come here alone, having assumed, apparently wrongly, that the rookie was with Ice at the hospital.

He jogged over to the squad, his stomach knotting painfully. Someone was sitting inside, head resting against the passenger-side window as if the person waiting was taking a nap. The guy had light hair, much like Wesley's, but he couldn't see his face clearly to make a positive identification.

It was hard to imagine the rookie would risk sleeping on the job. He may not have done everything the way he should have, but even he wouldn't be that clueless.

As he opened the door, the person inside toppled out of the squad, hitting the asphalt road with a hard thud. The rookie's pale white face pointed to the sky.

And above the rookie's dead stare was a small round bullet hole.

Wesley Durango had been murdered!

Made in the USA
Middletown, DE
14 July 2023